Let's Enjoy ... 1

The Christmas Stories

聖誕故事

The Gift of the Magi・聖誕禮物

The Fir Tree・樅樹

Original Authors O. Henry / Hans Christian Andersen
Adaptors Louise Benette / David Hwang
Illustrator Ludmila Pipchenko

WORDS 350

Let's Enjoy Masterpieces!

All the beautiful fairy tales and masterpieces that you have encountered during your childhood remain as warm memories in your adulthood. This time, let's indulge in the world of masterpieces through English. You can enjoy the depth and beauty of original works, which you can't enjoy through Chinese translations.

The stories are easy for you to understand because of your familiarity with them. When you enjoy reading, your ability to understand English will also rapidly improve.

This series of ***Let's Enjoy Masterpieces*** is a special reading comprehension booster program, devised to improve reading comprehension for beginners whose command of English is not satisfactory, or who are elementary, middle, and high school students. With this program, you can enjoy reading masterpieces in English with fun and efficiency.

This carefully planned program is composed of 5 levels, from the beginner level of 350 words to the intermediate and advanced levels of 1,000 words. With this program's level-by-level system, you are able to read famous texts in English and to savor the true pleasure of the world's language.

The program is well conceived, composed of reader-friendly explanations of English expressions and grammar, quizzes to help the student learn vocabulary and understand the meaning of the texts, and fabulous illustrations that adorn every page. In addition, with our "Guide to Listening," not only is reading comprehension enhanced but also listening comprehension skills are highlighted.

In the audio recording of the book, texts are vividly read by professional American actors. The texts are rewritten, according to the levels of the readers by an expert editorial staff of native speakers, on the basis of standard American English with the ministry of education recommended vocabulary. Therefore, it will be of great help even for all the students that want to learn English.

Please indulge yourself in the fun of reading and listening to English through ***Let's Enjoy Masterpieces***.

Introduction

歐·亨利 William S. Porter (O. Henry) (1862-1910)

Born William Sidney Porter, a prolific American short story writer and a master of surprise endings, is better known under his pen name "O. Henry." It is believed that the name was derived from his frequent calling of"Oh, Henry!" after the family cat.

O. Henry was born September 11, 1862 in North Carolina, where he spent his childhood. When William was three, his mother died, and he was raised by his paternal grandmother and aunt. His only formal education was received at the school of his Aunt Lina, where he developed a lifelong love of books.

William was an avid reader, but he left school at the age of fifteen. Then, he relocated to Texas and took a number of different jobs over the next several years, including pharmacist, draftsman, journalist, and bank teller, to help him to survive.

Then, in 1897 Porter was found guilty of the banking charges and sentenced to five years in prison. In 1898 he entered a prison at Columbus, Ohio, where he first started writing short stories based on his experiences.

Three years and about a dozen short stories later, he emerged from prison as "O. Henry" to help shield his true identity. Upon his release on July 24, 1901, he settled in

New York City and started to write full time. Over just ten years, he wrote about 300 short stories and gained worldwide acclaim as America's favorite short story writer.

As seen in his major stories, *The Last Leaf* and *The Gift of the Magi*, O. Henry usually wrote about the joys and sorrows of the lives of poor ordinary people in the Southern part of America and the slums of New York City. Typical for O. Henry's stories is a twist of plot that turns on an ironic or coincidental circumstance.

The Gift of the Magi is a Christmas story about a poor couple who loves each other. They want to buy a special Christmas gift for each other, but they do not have enough money, so they decide to sell their personal treasures to buy a gift. The wife cuts her hair, which is her pride, and sells it to buy a watch fob for her husband. And the husband sells his gold watch, which he values very much, to buy a hair ornament that would adorn his wife's beautiful hair.

In the title of this story, *The Gift of the Magi*, the Magi refer to the Three Wise Men who brought gifts to the baby Jesus. Each person reading the story reflects on the true spirit of Christmas and the love enjoyed by the couple who secretly sacrificed their greatest treasures to get gifts for each other. This implies the deeds performed by the Three Wise Men, who in turn become Magi themselves.

Introduction

安徒生 Hans Christian Andersen (1805-1875)

Hans Christian Andersen was born in Odense, a small fishing village, on the island of Funen, Denmark, on April 2, 1805. His father was a poor cobbler. Even so, he was a literary man of progressive idea, who enjoyed reading and encouraged Andersen to cultivate his artistic interests.

Andersen started writing when he was a university student. After his first novel *Improvisatore*, which was based on his trip to Italy in 1833, received critical acclaim,

Andersen earned even greater fame as a writer with his first book of fairy tales, *Tales Told for Children*. Later, Anderson became a well-loved writer of children's literature. By the time of his death in 1875, he had published a total of around 130 tales.

Andersen wrote many books that have been considered as the best works of literature for children, such as *The Little Mermaid*, *The Ugly Duckling*, and *The Emperor's New Clothes*. Despite many difficulties, Andersen rose above them to tell us enchanting stories.

In his works, Anderson zealously intertwined his lyrical writing style with manifestations of beautiful imaginary lands and humanism.

After living a solitary life, Andersen died alone. On his funeral day, all the Danish people wore mourning clothes, and the king and queen attended his funeral. Andersen was also an active poet. His beautiful poems and fairy tales are still loved by people around the world.

The Fir Tree is about a little fir tree that is always discontented and hopes for more.

After having longed to leave its boring forest home, the little fir tree finally achieves its wish, to be a Christmas tree, experiencing the dazzling grandeur of a Christmas night.

However, after the festivities of Christmas, the fir tree finds itself abandoned in the attic. As the days pass, it grows lonely.

One day, after realizing it had the happiest moments in its bland but pleasant forest life, the fir tree promises to appreciate little happiness in its present circumstances. However, it is too late.

This fairy tale, written in the form of a fable, teaches us a small lesson in life.

How to Use This Book

本書使用說明

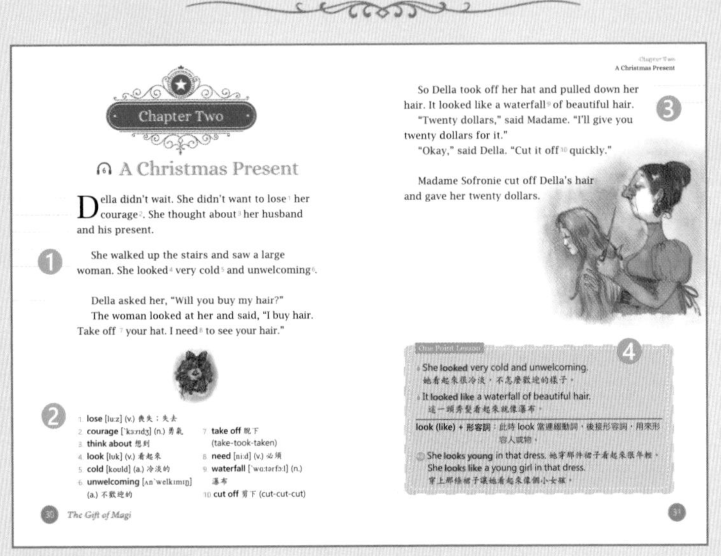

Chapter Two
A Christmas Present

Chapter Two

A Christmas Present

Della didn't wait. She didn't want to lose[1] her courage[2]. She thought about[3] her husband and his present.

She walked up the stairs and saw a large woman. She looked[4] very cold[5] and unwelcoming[6].

Della asked her, "Will you buy my hair?"
The woman looked at her and said, "I buy hair. Take off[7] your hat. I need[8] to see your hair."

1. lose [luːz] (v.) 喪失；失去
2. courage [ˋkɜːrɪdʒ] (n.) 勇氣
3. think about 想到
4. look [luk] (v.) 看起來
5. cold [kould] (a.) 冷淡的
6. unwelcoming [ʌnˋwelkɪmɪŋ] (a.) 不歡迎的
7. take off 脫下 (take-took-taken)
8. need [niːd] (v.) 必須
9. waterfall [ˋwɑːtərfɔːl] (n.) 瀑布
10. cut off 剪下 (cut-cut-cut)

30 The Gift of Magi

So Della took off her hat and pulled down her hair. It looked like a waterfall[9] of beautiful hair.
"Twenty dollars," said Madame. "I'll give you twenty dollars for it."
"Okay," said Della. "Cut it off[10] quickly."

Madame Sofronie cut off Della's hair and gave her twenty dollars.

One Point Lesson

- She looked very cold and unwelcoming.
  她看起來很冷淡，不怎麼歡迎的樣子。
- It looked like a waterfall of beautiful hair.
  這一頭秀髮看起來就像瀑布。

look (like) + 形容詞：此時 look 當連綴動詞，後接形容詞，用來形容人或物。

She looks young in that dress. 她穿那件裙子看起來很年輕。
She looks like a young girl in that dress.
穿上那條裙子讓她看起來像個小女孩。

31

1 Original English texts

It is easy to understand the meaning of the text, because the text is rewritten according to the levels of the readers.

2 Explanation of the vocabulary

The words and expressions that include vocabulary above the elementary level are clearly defined.

3 Response notes

Spaces are included in the book so you can take notes about what you don't understand or what you want to remember.

4 One point lesson

In-depth analyses of major grammar points and expressions help you to understand sentences with difficult grammar.

Audio Recording

In the audio recording, native speakers narrate the texts in standard American English. By combining the written words and the audio recording, you can listen to English with great ease.

Audio books have been popular in Britain and America for many decades. They allow the listener to experience the proper word pronunciation and sentence intonation that add important meaning and drama to spoken English. Students will benefit from listening to the recording twenty or more times.

After you are familiar with the text and recording, listen once more with your eyes closed to check your listening comprehension. Finally, after you can listen with your eyes closed and understand every word and every sentence, you are then ready to mimic the native speaker.

Then you should make a recording by reading the text yourself. Then play both recordings to compare your oral skills with those of a native speaker.

How to Improve Reading Ability

如何增進英文閱讀能力

1 *Catch key words*

Read the key words in the sentences and practice catching the gist of the meaning of the sentence. You might question how working with a few important words could enhance your reading ability. However, it's quite effective. If you continue to use this method, you will find out that the key words and your knowledge of people and situations enables you to understand the sentence.

2 *Divide long sentences*

Read in chunks of meaning, dividing sentences into meaningful chunks of information. In the book, chunks are arranged in sentences according to meaning. If you consider the sentences backwards or grammatically, your reading speed will be slow and you will find it difficult to listen to English.

You are ready to move to a more sophisticated level of comprehension when you find that narrowly focusing on chunks is irritating. Instead of considering the chunks, you will make it a habit to read the sentence from the beginning to the end to figure out the meaning of the whole.

3 Make inferences and assumptions

Making inferences and assumptions is part of your ability. If you don't know, try to guess the meaning of the words. Although you don't know all the words in context, don't go straight to the dictionary. Developing an ability to make inferences in the context is important.

The first way to figure out the meaning of a word is from its context. If you cannot make head or tail out of the meaning of a word, look at what comes before or after it. Ask yourself what can happen in such a situation. Make your best guess as to the word's meaning. Then check the explanations of the word in the book or look up the word in a dictionary.

4 Read a lot and reread the same book many times

There is no shortcut to mastering English. Only if you do a lot of reading will you make your way to the summit. Read fun and easy books with an average of less than one new word per page. Try to immerse yourself in English as often as you can.

Spend time "swimming" in English. Language learning research has shown that immersing yourself in English will help you improve your English, even though you may not be aware of what you're learning.

CONTENTS

The Fir Tree

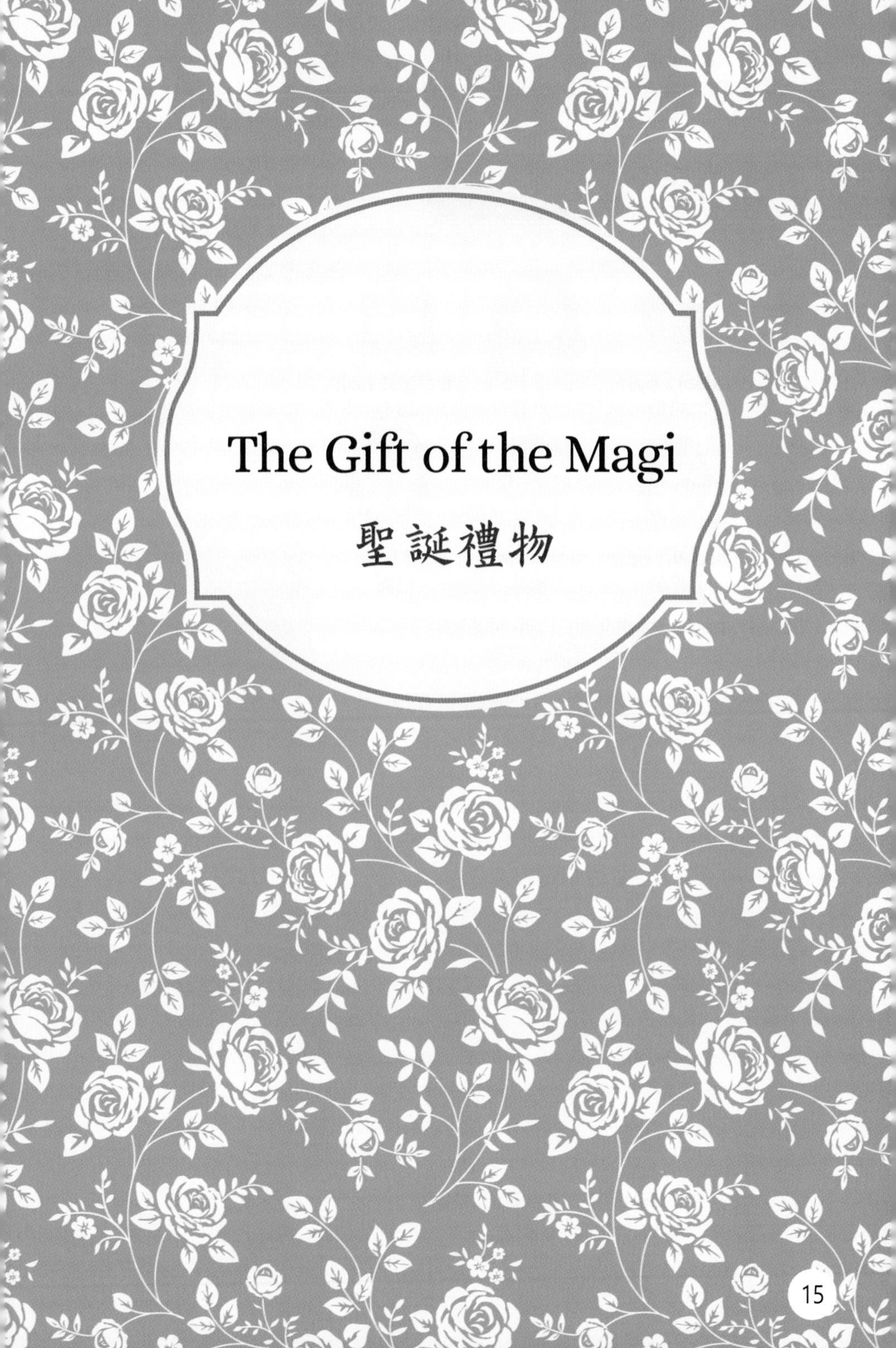

The Gift of the Magi

聖誕禮物

The Gift of the Magi

Before You Read

long hair 長髮

short hair 短髮

curly hair 捲髮

straight hair 直髮

blond hair 金髮

brown hair 棕髮

dark hair 黑髮

red hair 紅髮

She had a lot of long, beautiful hair.
她有一頭長而美麗的秀髮。

hurry down 迅速下樓

She hurried down the stairs.
她迅速地走下樓

stairs 樓梯

walk up 往上走

driveway/road 車道

sidewalk/pavement 人行道

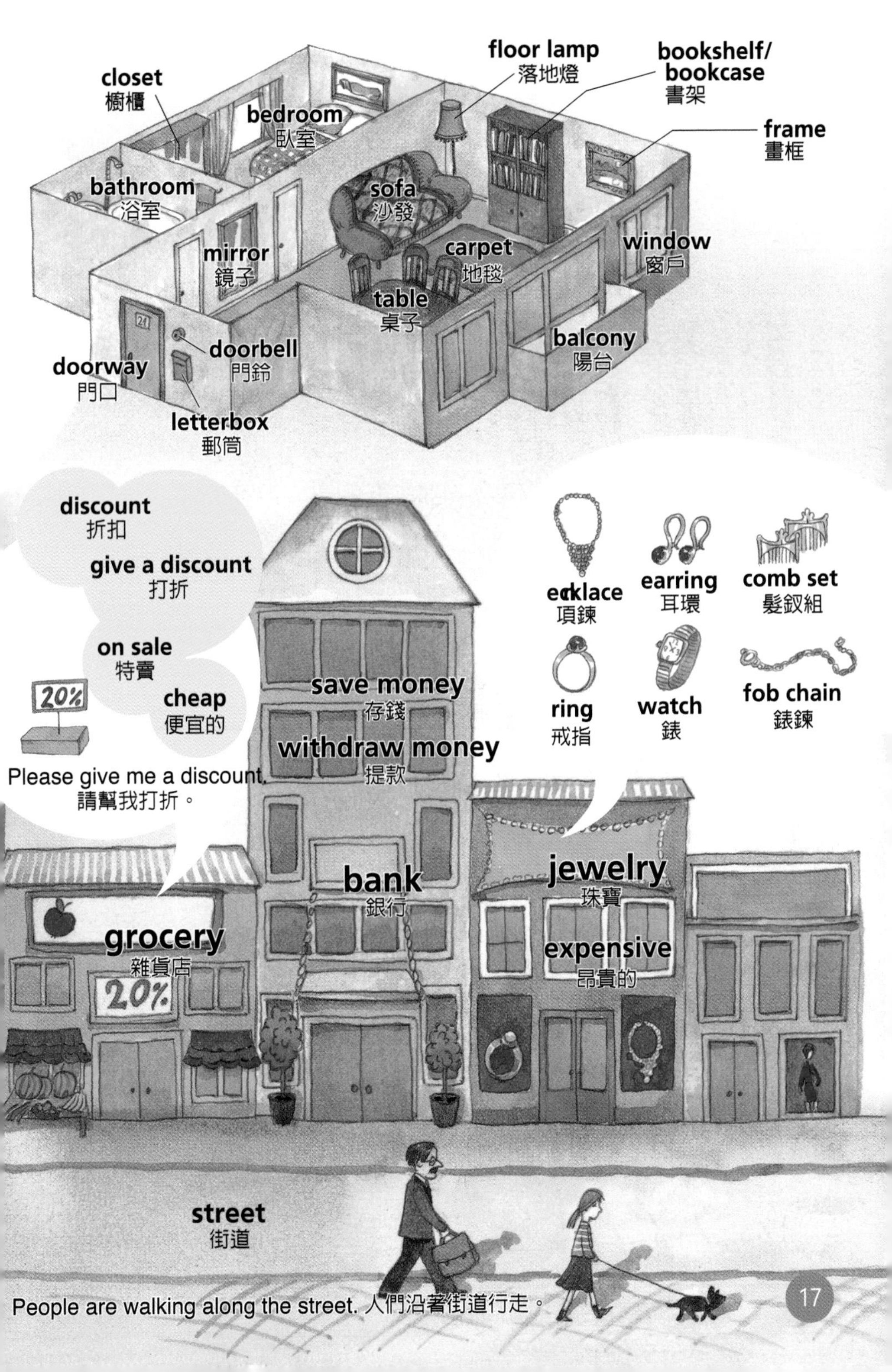

closet
櫥櫃
bedroom
臥室
floor lamp
落地燈
bookshelf/
bookcase
書架
frame
畫框
bathroom
浴室
sofa
沙發
mirror
鏡子
carpet
地毯
window
窗戶
table
桌子
balcony
陽台
doorbell
門鈴
doorway
門口
letterbox
郵筒
discount
折扣
give a discount
打折
on sale
特賣
cheap
便宜的
20%
Please give me a discount.
請幫我打折。
save money
存錢
withdraw money
提款
ecklace
項鍊
earring
耳環
comb set
髮釵組
ring
戒指
watch
錶
fob chain
錶鍊
jewelry
珠寶
bank
銀行
grocery
雜貨店
20%
expensive
昂貴的
street
街道
People are walking along the street. 人們沿著街道行走。

1 Only One Dollar and Eighty-Seven Cents

Della sat at[1] her kitchen table. She was counting[2] something. "One penny[3], two pennies, three pennies . . . ," she counted.

She was saving[4] pennies. Now, she had one dollar and eighty-seven cents.

She worked hard to save that money. Every time[5] she went to the grocery[6], she said, "Oh, it's too expensive! Please give me a discount[7]." She did this for many, many months.

She counted the money again and again. But there was only one dollar and eighty-seven cents. She cried out[8], "No! There must[9] be more money. I saved for so long[10]!"

1. **sit at . . .** 坐在……前
2. **count** [kaunt] (v.) 數；計算
3. **penny** [`peni] (n.) 分（美制錢幣單位）
4. **save** [seɪv] (v.) 存錢；儲蓄
5. **every time** 每一次
6. **grocery** [`grousəri] (n.) 雜貨店
7. **give a discount** 打折
8. **cry out** 大喊出來
9. **must** [mʌst] (aux.) 一定（表猜測之意）
10. **for so long** 如此長的時間

One Point Lesson

She was counting something.
她正在數著某樣東西。

be 動詞 + V-ing（現在分詞）：現在進行式，說明現在正在發生的事件。

e.g. Ellie was studying English.
艾莉正在讀英文。

2

Life[1] was not easy for Della. She lived in[2] a very small apartment. It cost[3] eight dollars a week. She had to spend[4] her money very wisely[5].

At the entrance[6] of the apartment, there was a doorbell[7]. But this didn't work[8] anymore. There was also a letterbox[9]. But it was too small for letters. It really wasn't a very good apartment.

On the letterbox, there was the name "Mr. James Dillingham Young." This was Della's husband.

1. **life** [laɪf] (n.) 生活
2. **live in . . .** 住在……
   (live-lived-lived)
3. **cost** [kɔ:st] (v.) 花費
   (cost-cost-cost)
4. **spend** [spend] (v.) 花費
5. **wisely** [`waɪzli] (adv.) 睿智地
6. **entrance** [`entrəns] (n.) 入口
7. **doorbell** [`dɔ:rbel] (n.) 門鈴
8. **work** [wɜ:rk] (v.) 運作
9. **letterbox** [`letərbɑ:ks] (n.) 信箱
10. **be proud of** 因……感到驕傲
11. **once** [wʌns] (adv.) 從前
12. **salary** [`sæləri] (n.) 薪水
13. **matter** [`mætər] (v.) 要緊
14. **greet** [gri:t] (v.) 歡迎；問候
15. **hug** [hʌg] (v.) 擁抱

A long time ago, Mr. James Dillingham Young was proud of [10] his name. Once [11], his salary [12] was thirty dollars a week. Now, it was only twenty.

Twenty dollars never bought very much. But, sometimes, that didn't matter [13]. When he came home, his wife always greeted [14] and hugged [15] him. He was her "Jim."

3

Now, Della still[1] sat at the kitchen table, and cried. She wiped[2] her tears[3] and stood up[4].

Tomorrow was Christmas. She only had one dollar and eighty-seven cents to buy her husband a present[5]. She saved for a long time but it wasn't enough[6]. She wanted to buy something very nice for him.

She walked to another window. As[7] she walked, she passed[8] a mirror. It was between two windows. It wasn't a very good mirror, of course. It was a mirror in an eight-dollar-a-week apartment. She looked at herself in the mirror. Her eyes were red and puffy[9] from[10] crying.

1. **still** [stɪl] (adv.) 依然
2. **wipe** [waɪp] (v.) 擦去；抹掉
3. **tear** [tɪr] (n.) 眼淚
4. **stand up** 站起來
5. **present** [`prezənt] (n.) 禮物
6. **enough** [ɪ`nʌf] (a.) 足夠的
7. **as** [əz] (adv.) 同時；當時
8. **pass** [pæs] (v.) 經過
9. **puffy** [`pʌfi] (a.) 腫的
10. **from** [frɑːm] (prep.) 由於

Then, she got an idea[1]. Her hair was tied up[2], but now she pulled it down[3]. She had a lot of very long, beautiful hair.

There were two things that she and her husband valued[4] very much.

One was a gold watch. Jim received it from his grandfather. He loved it very much.

1. **get an idea** 有個想法 (get-got-gotten)
2. **tie up** 綁起來
3. **pull down** 放下
4. **value** [ˋvælju:] (v.) 珍惜；重視
5. **envy** [ˋenvi] (v.) 嫉妒；羨慕
6. **than** [ðæn] (prep.) 用於比較級之後
7. **Queen of Sheba** 席巴女王，聖經中拜訪所羅門王並考驗其智慧。

The other was Della's hair. Della's hair was envied[5] by many people. Some people said to Della, "Your hair is more beautiful than[6] the Queen of Sheba's[7] jewels[8]!"

Jim's watch was also very wonderful[9]. Some people said to him, "Your watch is good enough for[10] a King!"

So, Jim and Della were very proud of these things.

8. **jewel** [`dʒu:ɪəl] (n.)
寶石；首飾

9. **wonderful** [`wʌndərfəl] (a.)
美妙的

10. **good enough for**
好得足以……

5

Della continued looking at her hair. It fell[1] around her shoulders, down her back, and to her knees. It was very, very long hair. Her hair was almost like[2] a dress.

She tied it up again. She did it quickly[3], but she suddenly[4] felt very sad. A couple of[5] tears rolled down[6] her cheeks.

1. **fall** [fɔ:l] (v.) 落下 (fall-fell-fallen)
2. **almost like** 幾乎像
3. **quickly** [`kwɪkli] (adv.) 迅速地
4. **suddenly** [`sʌdənli] (adv.) 突然地
5. **a couple of** 一些
6. **roll down** 滾落 (roll-rolled-rolled)
7. **put on** 穿上；戴上 (put-put-put)
8. **lock** [lɑ:k] (v.) 鎖上 (lock-locked-locked)
9. **hurry** [`hɜ:ri] (v.) 使加快；急速
10. **stair** [ster] (n.) 階梯；樓梯
11. **out of** 離開；在……之外
12. **look for** 尋找
13. **find** [faɪnd] (v.) 找到
14. **sign** [saɪn] (n.) 招牌
15. **goods** [gʊdz] (n.) 商品
16. **kind** [kaɪnd] (n.) 種類

She quickly put on[7] her old brown coat, and her old brown hat. She locked[8] her apartment and hurried[9] down the stairs[10] and out of[11] the apartment building.

She walked down the street to look for[12] a special store.

After a few minutes, she found[13] it and looked at the sign[14]: *Madame Sofronie. Hair Goods[15] of All Kinds[16].*

One Point Lesson

She **tied it up** again. 她又把它綁了起來。

動詞 + 副詞：動詞片語，若其受詞為代名詞，則一定要放在動詞與副詞之間。

e.g. ☑ Please, **turn it off**. 請關掉它。

e.g. ☒ Please, **turn off it**.

A Circle the words related to Della.

rich

discount

love

tear

poor

hair

hate

laughter

B Match.

❶ Door bell	•	•	ⓐ To do something quickly
❷ Letter box	•	•	ⓑ Be very smart
❸ Wise	•	•	ⓒ A thing to put mail into
❹ Hurry	•	•	ⓓ A thing to see yourself in
❺ Mirror	•	•	ⓔ A thing you press to make a noise

C True or False.

T F ❶ Jim received a watch from his father.

T F ❷ Della saved money for a long time.

T F ❸ It was easy for Della to save money.

T F ❹ Della's hair fell to her knees.

T F ❺ Jim had more money than before.

D Fill in the blanks with the given words.

envied valued loved

There were two things that she and her husband
❶ __________ very much. One was a gold watch.
Jim received it from his grandfather a long time ago.
He ❷ __________ it very much. The other was Della's hair.
Della's hair was ❸ __________ by many people.

Chapter Two

6 A Christmas Present

Della didn't wait. She didn't want to lose[1] her courage[2]. She thought about[3] her husband and his present.

She walked up the stairs and saw a large woman. She looked[4] very cold[5] and unwelcoming[6].

Della asked her, "Will you buy my hair?"

The woman looked at her and said, "I buy hair. Take off[7] your hat. I need[8] to see your hair."

1. **lose** [lu:z] (v.) 喪失；失去
2. **courage** [`kɜ:rɪdʒ] (n.) 勇氣
3. **think about** 想到
4. **look** [lʊk] (v.) 看起來
5. **cold** [kould] (a.) 冷淡的
6. **unwelcoming** [ʌn`welkəmɪŋ] (a.) 不歡迎的
7. **take off** 脫下 (take-took-taken)
8. **need** [ni:d] (v.) 必須
9. **waterfall** [`wɑ:tərfɔ:l] (n.) 瀑布
10. **cut off** 剪下 (cut-cut-cut)

So Della took off her hat and pulled down her hair. It looked like a waterfall[9] of beautiful hair.

"Twenty dollars," said Madame. "I'll give you twenty dollars for it."

"Okay," said Della. "Cut it off[10] quickly."

Madame Sofronie cut off Della's hair and gave her twenty dollars.

One Point Lesson

- She **looked** very cold and unwelcoming.
  她看起來很冷淡，不怎麼歡迎的樣子。
- It **looked like** a waterfall of beautiful hair.
  這一頭秀髮看起來就像瀑布。

look (like) + 形容詞：此時 look 當連綴動詞，後接形容詞，用來形容人或物。

e.g. She **looks young** in that dress. 她穿那件裙子看起來很年輕。
She **looks like** a young girl in that dress.
穿上那條裙子讓她看起來像個小女孩。

Della left the store happily. She went out to buy Jim's Christmas present.

For two hours, she searched[1] many stores. Finally[2], she found her husband's present. There was only one like it.

It was very simple but elegant[3]. It was a platinum[4] fob chain[5] for his watch.

1. **search** [sɜ:rtʃ] (v.) 尋找
2. **finally** [`faɪnəli] (adv.) 最後地
3. **elegant** [`eləgənt] (a.) 雅致的
4. **platinum** [`plætnəm] (n.) 白金
5. **fob chain** 錶帶
6. **perfect** [`pɜ:rfɪkt] (a.) 完美的
7. **gift** [gɪft] (n.) 禮物 (= present)
8. **pay for** 支付 (pay-paid-paid)
9. **regret** [rɪ`gret] (n.) 惋惜
10. **these days** 這些日子
11. **embarrassed** [ɪm`bærəst] (a.) 困窘的

It was the perfect[6] gift[7]. She paid twenty-one dollars for[8] it. She had no regrets[9]. Jim would love it. Jim loved his watch.

But these days[10], he was a little embarrassed[11]. He only looked at his watch in private[12]. It was because of the old leather[13] strap[14] on the watch.

Now, he could proudly[15] look at his watch. He won't have to be embarrassed anymore.

12. **in private** 私下
13. **leather** [ˋleðər] (n.) 皮革
14. **strap** [stræp] (n.) 繩；帶
15. **proudly** [ˋpraudli] (adv.) 自豪地

One Point Lesson

- It was **because of** the old leather strap on the watch.
  這是因為那個破舊的皮錶帶。

because 為從屬連接詞，後接子句。
because of 則因為介系詞 of，必須接名詞。

e.g. He couldn't come **because of** illness.
他因為生病，所以沒辦法來。

8

Della hurried[1] home with[2] her chain and eighty-seven cents. Now, she started to feel a little sad about her hair. But she thought, "It will grow[3] quickly."

She got out[4] her curling irons[5]. She turned her short hair into[6] many little curls[7]. She looked at her hair in the mirror again and again.

1. **hurry** [ˋhɜːri] (v.) 急速 (hurry-hurried-hurried)
2. **with** [wɪθ] (prep.) 帶著
3. **grow** [groʊ] (v.) 生長 (grow-grew-grown)
4. **get out** 拿出 (get-got-gotten)
5. **curling iron** 燙髮鉗
6. **turn . . . into** 把……變成
7. **curl** [kɜːrl] (n.)（一圈）捲髮

"I hope Jim doesn't hate[8] it," she thought. "I did it for him. I did it for love. What could I buy with[9] one dollar and eighty-seven cents? No! Jim won't hate it. He will think I look like a singing girl."

So, she forgot[10] about her hair. She started to prepare[11] dinner[12]. Tonight, they would have pork chops[13] and coffee.

8. **hate** [heɪt] (v.) 不喜歡；憎惡
9. **buy with . . .** 用……買 (buy-bought-bought)
10. **forget** [fər`get] (v.) 忘記 (forget-forgot-forgotten)
11. **prepare** [prɪ`per] (v.) 準備
12. **dinner** [`dɪnər] (n.) 晚餐
13. **pork chop** 豬排

9

Della heard him walking up the apartment stairs. Jim always came home on time[1].

She quickly sat down[2] on a chair near the doorway[3]. She put[4] the chain in her hand and made a little prayer[5], "Please, let[6] him think I am still beautiful!"

The door opened and her husband came in[7]. He looked very tired[8] tonight. He was only twenty-two, but he looked older[9]. He had many things to worry[10] about.

He took off[11] his old coat. He really needed a new one. Then, he saw his wife. His face had no expression[12].

Della thought, "What is he thinking? Does he hate my hair? Does he think I'm ugly?"

1. **on time** 準時
2. **sit down** 坐下 (sit-sat-sat)
3. **doorway** [`dɔ:rweɪ] (n.) 門口；入口
4. **put** [put] (v.) 放；置
5. **make a prayer** 祈禱；禱告
6. **let . . .** [let] (v.) 讓……
7. **come in** 進來
8. **tired** [taɪrd] (a.) 疲倦的
9. **older** [ouldər] (a.) 更老的
10. **worry (about)** 擔心
11. **take off** 脫下
12. **expression** [ɪk`spreʃən] (n.) 表情；臉色

One Point Lesson

"Please, **let him think** I am still beautiful!"
請讓他覺得我還是很美麗。

let + A + **動詞原形**：讓 A 做某事。

e.g. **Let me hold** your bag for you. 讓我為你拿袋子吧。

She could not wait for[1] him to speak. She jumped up[2] and ran to him.

"Jim, Honey[3]! Why don't you say something? Don't look like that. It'll grow quickly again. Don't worry! It grows very fast[4]," she said.

1. **wait for** 等待
2. **jump up** 跳起來
3. **honey** [`hʌni] (n.) 〔口語〕親愛的
4. **fast** [fæst] (adv.) 迅速地

"You cut your hair off?" he asked her. He seemed almost[5] stupid[6]. It was easy to see his wife's short hair.

"Yes," she said. "I cut it off and sold[7] it. I got[8] you a beautiful gift. I know you will love it. It's perfect for you. Do you hate my hair? I'm still the same[9] person. Don't you like me with or without[10] my hair?"

5. **almost** [ɔ:lmoust] (adv.) 差不多
6. **stupid** [`stu:pɪd] (a.) 愚蠢的
7. **sell** [sel] (v.) 賣 (sell-sold-sold)
8. **get** [get] (v.) 取得；得到
9. **same** [seɪm] (a.) 相同的
10. **with or without** 無論有沒有

One Point Lesson

Why don't you say something? 你怎麼不說句話？

Why don't you . . . ? 你何不……？

→ 否定疑問句，可用來詢問或提供建議。

e.g. Why don't you go to the doctor?
你怎麼不去看醫生呢？

Comprehension Quiz Chapter Two

A Fill in the blanks with proper words.

opened   walked   took   cut

❶ She __________ up the stairs.

❷ Della __________ off her hat.

❶ She __________ off Della's hair.

❹ He __________ the door and came in.

B Rewrite the sentences in simple past tense.

❶ Della sees them in a Broadway store window.

⇨ Della ______ them in a Broadway store window.

❷ She sits on a chair near the doorway.

⇨ She ______ on a chair near the doorway.

❸ She cannot wait for him to speak.

⇨ She ______________ for him to speak.

C Choose the correct answer.

1 What did she buy for Jim?

(a) A watch
(b) A coat
(c) A fob chain
(d) Shoes

2 Why did Della cut her hair off?

(a) Because she wanted to buy Jim a good present.
(b) Because short hair looked good on her.
(c) Because she didn't like her long hair anymore.
(d) Because Jim asked her to.

D Fill in the blanks with the given words.

regrets perfect dollars embarrassed

It was the 1 ___________ gift. She paid twenty one 2 ___________ for it. She had no 3 ___________. Jim would love it. Jim loved his watch. But these days, he was a little 4 ___________.

Chapter Three

The Big Surprise

Now, Jim looked at his wife. He said, "Come here. I want to hold[1] you."

Della walked to her husband and they held each other[2] for a few moments[3].

"Please don't misunderstand[4] me," he said. "Nothing[5] could stop me from loving you. No haircut[6] will change[7] that."

1. **hold** [hoʊld] (v.) 握住；緊握
2. **each other** 彼此
3. **for a few moments** 過了幾分鐘
4. **misunderstand** [ˋmɪsʌndərˋstænd] (v.) 誤會
5. **nothing** [ˋnʌθɪŋ] (n.) 無事；沒有什麼事
6. **haircut** [ˋherkʌt] (n.) 剪髮
7. **change** [tʃeɪndʒ] (v.) 改變
8. **take** [teɪk] (v.) 拿 (take-took-taken)

Then, he took[8] something from his pocket and put it on the table.

"Open the package[9]," he said. "Then you will know why I looked so strange. Go on, open it up."

She took the package and started to open it. A moment later[10], she screamed[11] happily, "Oh, Honey! It's beautiful." This happiness[12] soon changed to[13] tears. Della started to cry.

9. **package** [ˋpækɪdʒ] (n.) 包裹
10. **a moment later** 過了一會兒
11. **scream** [skriːm] (v.) 尖叫
12. **happiness** [ˋhæpɪnəs] (n.) 快樂；開心
13. **change to** 轉變成

One Point Lesson

Nothing could stop me from loving you.
沒有什麼能阻止我對你的愛。

「**stop . . . from + V-ing**」：阻止……去做……

e.g. Who could stop her from doing so?
誰能阻止她這麼做？

12

Her husband rushed[1] to her side[2]. "Don't cry," he said. "Don't cry."

But she couldn't stop. He comforted[3] her for a few minutes[4].

On the table, there was a set[5] of combs[6]. They were beautiful.

1. **rush** [rʌʃ] (v.) 速進；急進
2. **side** [saɪd] (n.) 身邊
3. **comfort** [ˋkʌmfərt] (v.) 安慰
4. **for a few minutes** 好幾分鐘
5. **set** [set] (n.) 一組；一套
6. **comb** [koum] (n.) 頭釵；梳子

Della saw them in a Broadway store window. She wanted them for a long time. They were very expensive. They would have looked beautiful in her long, brown hair.

She picked them up[7] and hugged[8] them. She looked at her husband and said happily, "I will wear[9] them soon. My hair grows[10] very fast."

Then, she remembered something. "Oh! Oh!" she cried. "I didn't give you your present yet."

She jumped up and opened her hand. Her eyes were now sparkling[12] with joy[13].

7. **pick up** 拿起來
8. **hug** [hʌg] (v.) 擁抱
9. **wear** [wer] (v.) 戴起來
10. **grow** [groʊ] (v.) 生長 (grow-grew-grown)
11. **sparkle** [ˋspɑːrkəl] (v.) 閃耀
12. **with joy** 帶著喜悅

"Isn't it beautiful? It will be perfect for your watch. I looked everywhere[1] for it today. Now you won't[2] be embarrassed about your watch. You can look at it one hundred times[3] a day. Give me your watch. I want to put it on your watch," she said.

But Jim did not give her his watch. Instead[4], he lay down[5] on the sofa and smiled.

1. **everywhere** [ˋevriwer] (adv.) 到處
2. **won't** 不會（will not 的縮寫）
3. **time** [taɪm] (n.) 次數
4. **instead** [inˋsted] (adv.) 代替；取代
5. **lie down** 坐下 (lie-lay-lain)
6. **anymore** [ˏeniˋmɔːr] (adv.) 再也
7. **put away** 放下 (put-put-put)
8. **believe** [bɪˋliːv] (v.) 相信

"Della," he said. "I don't want to think about Christmas and Christmas presents anymore[6]. Let's put them away[7]. Let's use them later."

"I don't have my watch anymore. I sold it to buy your combs. Why don't you make the dinner now?"

Della just looked at him. She couldn't believe[8] it. But she didn't say anything. She just went to the kitchen to prepare dinner.

One Point Lesson

I sold it **to buy** your combs.
我把它賣掉幫你買了髮釵。

本句中的 to 為介系詞，用於表示目的，後接動詞原形。

e.g. I studied hard **to pass** the exam.
我用功讀書是為了要通過考試。

14

People love to give gifts at Christmas. This tradition[1] began with[2] the Magi[3].

They were wise[4] men. They brought[5] gifts to baby Jesus[6] in the manger[7] a long time ago. They were wise men and their gifts were wise, too.

1. **tradition** [trə`dɪʃən] (n.) 傳統
2. **begin with . . .** 由……開始
3. **Magi** [`meɪdʒaɪ] (n.) 聖經中攜帶禮物祝賀耶穌降生的東方三賢士（magus 的複數）
4. **wise** [waɪz] (a.) 有智慧的
5. **bring** [brɪŋ] (v.) 帶來
6. **Jesus** [`dʒi:zəs] (n.) 耶穌
7. **manger** [`meɪndʒər] (n.) 飼料槽
8. **foolish** [`fu:lɪʃ] (a.) 愚蠢的
9. **give away** 送走
10. **precious** [`preʃəs] (a.) 珍貴的

This is a story of two foolish[8] people. They foolishly gave away[9] their most precious[10] things. But they did it for love. This is the reason[11] for giving gifts.

So those two foolish people were the wisest[12] of all. They are the Magi. They were poor[13], yet they were rich[14] in love. They sold their most precious things for each other. This is the true[15] meaning[16] of Christmas.

11. **reason** [ˋriːzən] (n.) 理由；原因
12. **wisest** 最聰明的（wise 的最高級）
13. **poor** [pʊr] (a.) 貧窮的
14. **rich** [rɪtʃ] (a.) 富有的
15. **true** [truː] (a.) 真實的
16. **meaning** [ˋmiːnɪŋ] (n.) 意義

A Circle the words related to Magi.

Christmas

three men

hate

sad

foolish

New Year's Day

gift

money

wise

B True or False.

T F ❶ Jim gave Della an expensive present.

T F ❷ She cried because she didn't like the present.

T F ❸ Jim sold his watch to buy her a present.

T F ❹ Jim was angry about Della's hair.

T F ❺ People only want to get a gift at Christmas.

C Rewrite the sentences in past continuous tense.

Jim looked at his wife. ⇨ Jim was looking at his wife.

1. He took something from his pocket.
   ⇨ He ______________ something from his pocket.
2. My hair grows fast.
   ⇨ My hair ______________ fast.
3. Jim didn't give her his watch.
   ⇨ Jim ______________ her his watch.
4. She went to the kitchen to prepare for dinner.
   ⇨ She ______________ to the kitchen to prepare for dinner.

D Rearrange the sentences in chronological order.

1. Jim said, "I sold the watch to buy your combs."
2. Jim gave Della a package to open.
3. Della went to the kitchen to prepare dinner.
4. Della said, "Now you won't be embarrassed about your watch."

_______ ⇨ _______ ⇨ _______ ⇨ _______

The Fir Tree

樅樹

The Fir Tree

Before You Read

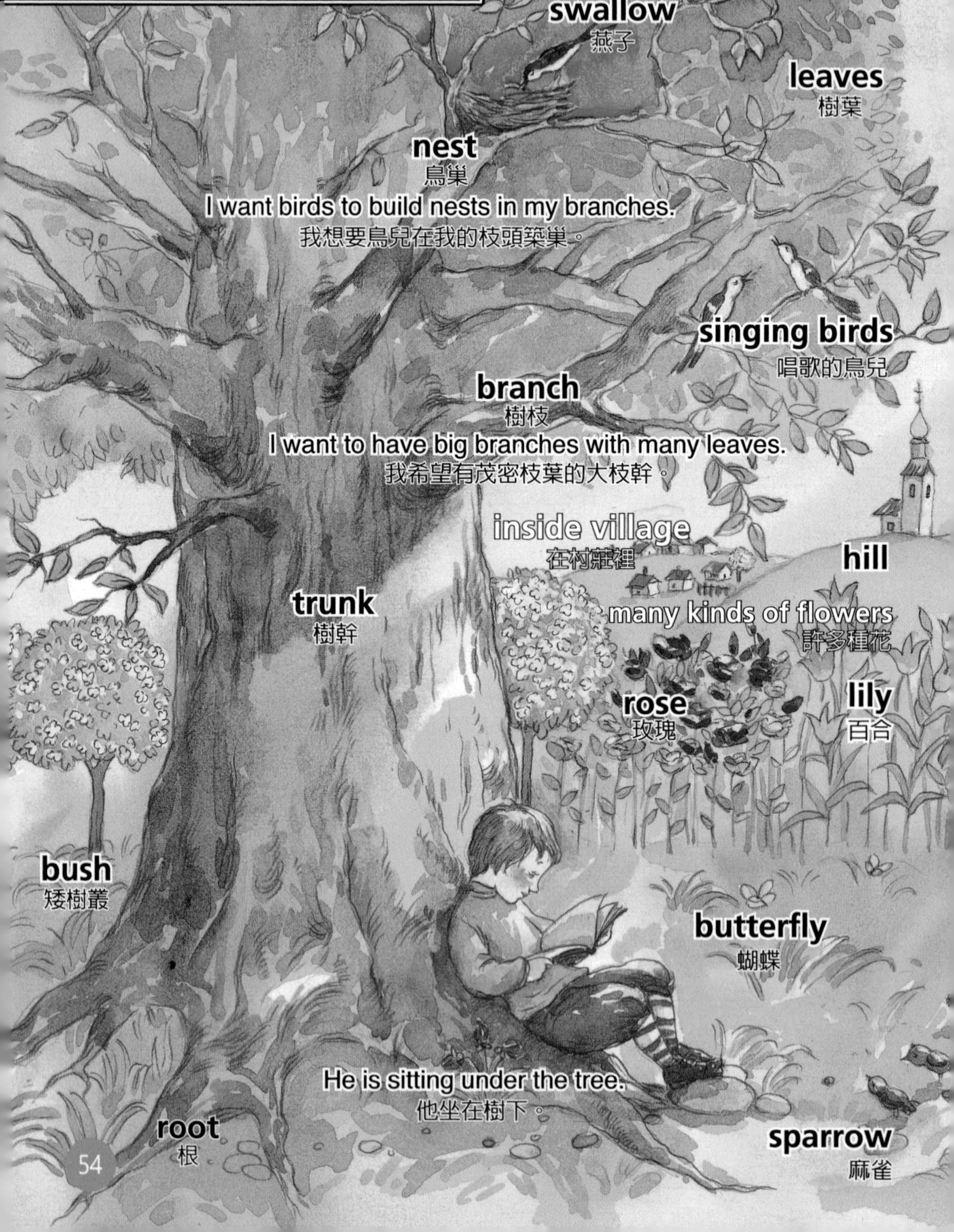

swallow
燕子

leaves
樹葉

nest
鳥巢
I want birds to build nests in my branches.
我想要鳥兒在我的枝頭築巢。

singing birds
唱歌的鳥兒

branch
樹枝
I want to have big branches with many leaves.
我希望有茂密枝葉的大枝幹。

inside village
在村莊裡

hill

trunk
樹幹

many kinds of flowers
許多種花

rose
玫瑰

lily
百合

bush
矮樹叢

butterfly
蝴蝶

He is sitting under the tree.
他坐在樹下。

root
根

sparrow
麻雀

sky
天空
warm sunlight
溫暖的陽光
sun
太陽
flying birds
飛鳥
rainy
下雨的
snowy
下雪的
sunny
晴朗的
windy
刮風的
a lot of sunshine and fresh air
大量的陽光與新鮮空氣
woods/forest
森林
carnation
康乃馨
pine tree
松樹
This pine tree is much bigger than the fir trees.
松樹比樅樹高大的多。
outside village
村莊外
tulip
鬱金香
fir tree
樅樹
These two fir trees are the same size.
這兩棵樅樹一樣大。
grass
草地
pick
摘
strawberry
草莓
Many children came to pick strawberries in the woods.
許多孩子到森林裡採草莓。

Chapter One

The Tree in the Forest

Just outside[1] a village, there was a beautiful forest. It was full of[2] so many kinds of[3] trees.

On the edge[4] of the forest, there was a pretty Fir tree[5]. He was still a small tree. He lived in a very nice place. There was a lot of[6] sunshine and fresh air.

1. **outside** [ˌaut`saɪd] (prep.) 在……之外
2. **be full of** 充滿
3. **many kinds of . . .** 許多種類的……
4. **edge** [ɛdʒ] (n.) 邊緣；邊界
5. **fir tree** 樅樹
6. **a lot of** 很多
7. **pine tree** 松樹
8. **want to be** 想要成為
9. **care about** 在乎；關心

Around him, there were many other fir trees. Some were much bigger and others were the same size. There were also many pine trees[7]. They all looked so big. He wanted to be[8] big too.

His life was very good. But he did not know that. He did not care about[9] the warm sunshine or fresh air.

One Point Lesson

Some were much bigger and **others** were the same size.
有一些高大得多，也有一些是同樣的大小。

Some . . . others . . . : 一些……；其他的……
One . . . the others . . . : 其中一個……；剩下的……

e.g. **One** left, and **the others** stayed.
有一個人離開了，剩下的都留下來。

16

Many children[1] came to pick[2] strawberries[3] in the woods[4]. Sometimes, they sat under the little Fir tree. They often[5] said, "Let's sit under that little Fir tree. It is so pretty."

1. **children** [`tʃɪldrən] (n.) 兒童（child 的複數）
2. **pick** [pɪk] (v.) 摘；採
3. **strawberry** [`strɔ:bəri] (n.) 草莓
4. **woods** [wʊdz] (n.) 森林 (= forest)

But the Fir tree did not like this. He did not like being 'little.'

Every year, the Fir tree grew[6] bigger. But he was still not happy. He looked at other trees around him.

He thought, "I want to be big like those trees.
I want to have big branches[7] with many leaves[8].
I want to stand tall, and see many things in the sky.
I want birds to build[9] nests[10] in my branches.
I want to bend[11] elegantly[12] in the wind."

He was never happy.

5. **often** [`ɔ:fən] (adv.) 常常
6. **grow** [grou](v.) 生長
7. **branch** [bræntʃ] (n.) 枝；樹枝
8. **leaf** [li:f] (n.) 樹葉
9. **build** [bɪld] (v.) 建造 (build-built-built)
10. **nest** [nest] (n.) 鳥巢
11. **bend** [bend] (v.) 彎曲
12. **elegantly** [`eləgəntli] (adv.) 高雅地

17

Two more years went by[1] and he grew and grew. He was now much[2] bigger.

"I am getting bigger," he thought. "Grow! I must grow taller!"

Every autumn[3], the woodcutters[4] came to cut down[5] the largest trees.

The Fir tree heard the sounds "Chop[6]! Chop! Chop!"

Then, there was a "Crash[7]!" The trees tumbled down[8]. The Fir tree became very frightened[9].

1. **go by**（時間）過去 (go-went-gone)
2. **much** [mʌtʃ] (adv.) 更加
3. **autumn** [`ɔ:təm] (n.) 秋天 (= fall)
4. **woodcutter** [`wʊdˏkʌtər] (n.) 樵夫
5. **cut down** 砍下
6. **chop** [tʃɑ:p] (v.) 劈；砍
7. **crash** [kræʃ] (n.) 巨大的聲響
8. **tumble down** 墜下；猛跌
9. **frightened** [`fraɪtənd] (a.) 驚恐的
10. **think** [θɪŋk] (v.) 想 (think-thought-thought)
11. **happen** [`hæpən] (v.) 發生

The Fir tree thought[10], "Why did the men cut down the trees?

Where did they go?

What will happen[11] to them?"

One Point Lesson

I'm **getting bigger**. 我正在長大。

get + 形容詞：表示「變成」，get 為連綴動詞。

e.g. I'm **getting better**. 我覺得好多了。

18

He saw some swallows[1], and asked them.

"Yes, I think I saw them," they answered. I flew[2] to Egypt[3] and I saw many ships. On the ships, there were gigantic[4] masts[5]. They had huge[6] white sails[7] and danced in the wind. They were very elegant[8]. You should[9] be proud[10]."

1. **swallow** [`swɑ:lou] (n.) 燕子
2. **fly** [flaɪ] (v.) 飛 (fly-flew-flown)
3. **Egypt** [`ɪ:dʒɪpt] (n.) 埃及
4. **gigantic** [ˏdʒaɪ`gæntɪk] (n.) 巨大的
5. **mast** [mæst] (n.) 船桅
6. **huge** [hju:dʒ] (a.) 極大的
7. **sail** [seɪl] (n.) 帆
8. **elegant** [`eləgənt] (a.) 優雅的
9. **should** [ʃud] (aux.) 應該
10. **proud** [praud] (a.) 驕傲的

This made the Fir tree happy. He thought, "I want to sail[11] across[12] the sea. I want to be a gigantic mast with dancing sails. I would be so happy."

The air and the sunshine heard the tree and said, "Don't wish[13] for another life. Be happy now. You have warm sunlight. You have a healthy[14] trunk[15]." But the tree did not understand them.

11. **sail** [seɪl] (v.) 航行
12. **across** [ə`krɔ:s] (prep.) 橫過；穿過
13. **wish** [wɪʃ] (v.) 希望
14. **healthy** [`helθi] (a.) 健康的
15. **trunk** [trʌŋk] (n.) 樹幹

One Point Lesson

This made the Fir tree happy. 這讓樅樹非常開心。

「**make** + 受詞 + 形容詞 / 名詞補語」：用來表示對人或物造成如何的效果。

e.g. The news made my father sick.
這個消息讓我父親覺得反感。

This year, the woodcutters came before Christmas. They did not cut down big trees. They cut down young trees.

The Fir tree was very confused[1]. "Why are they cutting down such[2] young trees?"

There were some sparrows[3] sitting in his branches. So the Fir tree asked them, "Where are the trees going? Those are smaller[4] than[5] me. Why did the men cut them down?"

1. **confused** [kɪn`fju:zd] (a.) 困惑的
2. **such** [sʌtʃ] (a.) 如此的；這樣的
3. **sparrow** [`spæroʊ] (n.) 麻雀
4. **smaller** [`smɔ:lər] (a.) 更小的（small 的比較級）
5. **than** [ðæn] (prep.) 與……相較

One Point Lesson

There were some sparrows **sitting** in his branches.
有幾隻麻雀停在他的樹枝上。

V-ing（現在分詞）可以像關係子句一樣，放在名詞或代名詞後面做修飾。

e.g. I know the girl **singing** beautifully.
我認識那個歌聲很美的女生。

20

This time[1], the Sparrows said, "We know! We looked in through[2] some windows in the village. The trees will go there. They will be so beautiful. They will wear so many colors[3] and lights[4]. They will be so happy. They will live in a warm room with many presents[5] under them."

1. **this time** 這一次
2. **through** [θruː] (prep.) 穿過；透過
3. **color** [ˋkʌlər] (n.) 顏色
4. **light** [laɪt] (n.) 燈
5. **present** [ˋprezənt] (n.) 禮物
6. **be interested in . . .** 對……有興趣
7. **sound** [saʊnd] (v.) 聽起來
8. **better than . . .** 比……更好
9. **such a place** 這樣的地方
10. **suffer** [ˋsʌfər] (v.) 受苦
11. **must be** 一定是
12. **the best** 最好的；最佳的
13. **ignore** [ɪgˋnɔːr] (v.) 忽略；不理睬

The Fir tree was very interested in[6] this. The tree thought, "It sounds[7] wonderful. It is better than[8] sailing across the sea. I want to live in such a place[9]. I suffer[10] so much in this forest! Something better must be[11] waiting for me."

Again, the sunlight and the air heard the tree. They said to him, "Do not be so foolish. Your life in the forest is the best[12]. Be happy with that." But the tree ignored[13] them.

One Point Lesson

Something better must be waiting for me.
一定有更好的生活在等著我。

something, anything, nothing ：修飾 something、anything 和 nothing 的形容詞必須放在後面。

e.g. Do you want **something cold**?
你想要來點冷的食物嗎？
There's **nothing special** about this party.
這個舞會沒什麼特別的。

Finally[1], the woodcutters came. They stood in front of[2] him, and said, "This one will be perfect[3]."

A few moments later, the tree felt a sharp[4] pain[5]. It was the ax[6]. Whack[7]! Whack! Whack! He fell to[8] the ground[9]. Crash!

It was not the happiness he dreamed of[10]. He suddenly felt very sad.

He thought, "My home! I am separated from[11] my home. I will never see it again. I will never feel the fresh air or the warm sunlight. I will never hear the birds sing again. I am so sad."

1. **finally** [ˋfaɪnəli] (adv.) 終於；最後
2. **in front of . . .** 在⋯⋯前面
3. **perfect** [ˋpɜːrfɪkt] (a.) 完美的
4. **sharp** [ʃɑːrp] (a.) 劇烈的
5. **pain** [peɪn] (n.) 痛苦
6. **ax** [æks] (n.) 斧頭
7. **whack** [wæk] (n.) 重擊
8. **fall to** 跌落至 (fall-fell-fallen)
9. **ground** [graʊnd] (n.) 地面；土地
10. **dream of** 夢想
11. **be separated from . . .** 與⋯⋯分開

A Fill in the blanks with the given words.

cuts pick flies sits

1. Children came to _____ strawberries.

2. A man _____ under a tree.

3. He _____ down the tree.

4. A bird _____ to their nest.

B True or False.

T F 1. The Fir tree was unhappy living in the forest.

T F 2. The Fir tree always wanted to be big.

T F 3. The air and the sunshine hated him.

T F 4. Men went to the forest to plant new trees.

C Fill in the blanks with "many" or "much."

There were many students.

I don't have much homework.

1. There aren't __________ books on the table.
2. You don't need __________ money?
3. There isn't __________ milk.
4. There weren't __________ balloons left after the party.

D Rearrange the sentences in chronological order.

1. Woodcutters cut down the Fir tree.
2. Many children went to the woods to pick strawberries.
3. The Fir tree was sad when he left the forest.
4. The Fir tree wanted to sail across the sea.
5. Woodcutters came to cut down very big trees.

________ ⇨ ________ ⇨ ________ ⇨ ________ ⇨ ________

Before You Read

a large golden star
金色的大星星

church
教堂

curtain
窗簾

window
窗戶

sled
雪橇

Rudolph
馴鹿魯道夫

apple
蘋果

Christmas tree
聖誕樹

They hung many colored decorations on the tree.
他們在樹上掛許多各色裝飾品。

Fir tree
樅樹

Santa Clause
聖誕老人

give a present
送禮

present/gift
禮物

many presents under the tree
樹下有許多禮物

get / receive a present
收到禮物

Christmas decorations
聖誕飾品
wreath
花圈
a large, warm room
一個大又溫暖的房間
angel
天使
bell
鈴鐺
snow man
雪人
fire place
火爐
socks/stockings
襪子
sofa
沙發
The children screamed joyfully.
孩子們歡樂地喧鬧吼叫。
candle 蠟燭
Christmas pudding/cake/cookie
聖誕布丁／蛋糕／餅乾
Children will laugh and play next to the tree.
孩子們會在樹旁嬉笑玩樂。

Chapter Two

A Very Sad Life

The Fir tree was put into[1] a large room. He looked around[2] the room curiously[3]. Soon after[4], many servants[5] and young girls came in[6].

They started to decorate[7] the tree. They hung[8] many colored decorations[9] on the tree. On the top[10], they put a large golden star.

The tree looked at his branches. He was dressed in[11] many colors. He looked very beautiful.

"Now my life will be wonderful," thought the tree. "I will live my life in this warm room. The sunlight and the air were all wrong. Maybe the sparrows will come to see me. Maybe they will tell other trees about my grand[12] life."

He was so happy now. He felt very good about his future.

1. **be put into** 放進
2. **look around** 環視四周
3. **curiously** [`kjʊriəsli] (adv.) 好奇地
4. **soon after** 不久後
5. **servant** [`sɜ:rvənt] (n.) 僕人
6. **come in** 進來
7. **decorate** [`dekəreɪt] (v.) 裝飾
8. **hang** [hæŋ] (v.) 掛 (hang-hung-hung)
9. **decoration** [`dekə͵reɪʃən] (n.) 裝飾
10. **top** [tɑ:p] (n.) 頂端；最高部分
11. **be dressed in** 以……裝飾
12. **grand** [grænd] (a.) 華麗的；偉大的

23

A few moments later, the door to the room opened. Many children came in. They ran to the tree and stopped. Just after them, the adults[1] walked in. Together, they all admired[2] the beautiful tree. The tree felt so happy.

It was very noisy[3] in that room that night. The children screamed[4] joyfully[5] and danced around the tree.

1. **adult** [ə`dʌlt] (n.) 大人
2. **admire** [əd`maɪr] (v.) 欣賞
3. **noisy** [`nɔɪzi] (a.) 吵鬧的
4 **scream** [skriːm] (v.) 尖叫
5. **joyfully** [`dʒɔɪfəli] (adv.) 喜悅地
6. **content** [`kənˌtent] (a.) 滿足的

Later, all the people sang Christmas carols together. The tree enjoyed watching all of this. He thought, “This is all for me! I will enjoy this every night.” He was very content[7].

One Point Lesson

The tree enjoyed watching all of this.
樹開心地看著這一切。

enjoy：享受；喜歡，後面須接受詞，受詞必須是名詞或動名詞。

e.g. My friend, Gina, **enjoys taking** a walk.
我朋友吉娜很喜歡散步。

24

The next morning[1], the tree wanted to see the children. But they did not come to see him.

Instead[2], some servants came into[3] the room. He thought, "Yesterday, the servants decorated me. Today, they will decorate me again." But this did not happen[4].

The servants pulled the tree down[5]. They took him out of[6] the room. Then, they took him up many stairs[7] and put him into a dark room. He was forgotten[8].

1. **next morning** 第二天早上
2. **instead** [ɪn`sted] (adv.) 相反地
3. **come into** 進來
4. **happen** [`hæpən] (v.) 發生
5. **pull A down** 把 A 拉倒
6. **take out of . . .** 帶出……
(take-took-taken)
7. **stairs** [sterz] (n.) 階梯；樓梯
8. **be forgotten** 被遺忘
9. **pass** [pæs] (v.) 經過
10. **squeak** [skwi:k] (n.)
短促尖銳的聲音
11. **mice** [maɪs] (n.) 老鼠
（mouse 的複數）

Many more lonely nights passed[9].

One night, there was a sound, "Squeak[10]! Squeak!" They were little mice[11]. The curious[12] mice wanted to know about[13] the tree.

The tree told stories about the forest. They were amazed[14]. They said, "Your life is interesting! You were very happy in the forest!"

The tree replied, "Yes, I was happy there. But my life is not interesting anymore."

12. **curious** [`kjʊriəs] (a.) 好奇的
13. **know about** 了解
14. **amazed** [ə`meɪzd] (a.) 驚異的

25

At night they went to hear his story. He told them many stories about Christmas Eve. This continued[1] for a few[2] more nights.

Finally, the tree had no more stories and had to tell the same stories over.

The mice thought, "Maybe the stories are not very interesting after all[3]." So, the mice did not go to the tree at night.

1. **continue** [kən`tɪnjuː] (v.) 繼續
2. **a few** 一些
3. **after all** 畢竟；終究
4. **visit** [`vɪzɪt] (v.) 拜訪
5. **listen to** 聆聽
6. **must** [mʌst] (aux.) 必須
7. **careful** [`kerfəl] (a.) 小心的
8. **leave** [liːv] (v.) 離開

It became very lonely in that dark room. "Why don't the mice come to visit[4] me?" he thought.

"It was better when the mice came to listen to[5] me. I must[6] enjoy those happy times more. I will be careful[7] next time. When I leave[8] this room, I will really enjoy everything. But when will that be?"

One Point Lesson

When I leave this room, I will really enjoy everything.
等我離開這個房間，我要好好享受每一件事。

when：指「一旦」，代表未來預計會發生的事，但此時 when 子句裡不用未來式。

e.g. When you tell me your secret, I'll tell you mine.
等你告訴我你的秘密，我就告訴你我的秘密。

26

One day[1], the door to that dark, lonely room opened. Many people came in.

"At last," thought the tree. "They come to give me a new life."

One man came and pushed the tree down[2] onto[3] the floor[4]. Ouch[5]! The tree landed[6] very heavily[7]. Then two servants picked up[8] the tree and took it outside[9].

Now the tree was lying[10] in the sunlight. "This is wonderful. My new life is beginning. It is spring now. They will plant[11] me and I will grow."

The tree really enjoyed the fresh air. He looked around at the garden[12]. It was so beautiful. There were roses and carnations[13]. He saw many birds flying in the garden. It was a wonderful day for the tree.

1. **one day** 一天
2. **push down** 推倒
3. **onto** 在……之上
4. **floor** [flɔ:r] (n.) 地面
5. **ouch** [aʊtʃ] (int.) 唉唷
6. **land** [lænd] (v.) 著地
7. **heavily** [`hevɪli] (adv.) 重重地
8. **pick up** 拾起
9. **outside** [`aʊtˏsaɪd] (adv.) 在外面地
10. **lie** [laɪ] (v.) 躺臥；橫放 (lie-lay-lain)
11. **plant** [plænt] (v.) 種植
12. **garden** [`gɑ:rdən] (n.) 花園
13. **carnation** [kɑ:r`neɪʃən] (n.) 康乃馨

One Point Lesson

The tree landed very heavily. 樹重重地倒在地上。

1. The man | landed | the tree | very heavily.
2. The tree | was landed | very heavily | (by the man).

第二句為被動式，與第一句的意義相同，句尾 by the man 中的 the man 因對象不明確，故可以省略。

27

The tree relaxed[1] in the sunlight, and spread out[2] his branches.

Just then[3], he discovered[4] something terrible. He couldn't move[5] his branches. He looked at them and was shocked[6]. They were all yellow. His branches were weak[7]. He was a very sad tree now.

Some children were running around the garden.

They cried, "Look! It is the Christmas tree. It is so old and ugly[8]. But look! It still has the yellow star on top of it."

One of the children took the star from the tree. The children didn't care about[9] the old tree. There was nothing[10] beautiful about the tree anymore.

1. **relax** [rɪ`læks] (v.) 放鬆
2. **spread out** 散布 [spred]
3. **just then** 就在那時
4. **discover** [dɪ`skʌvər] (v.) 發現
5. **move** [mu:v] (v.) 移動
6. **be shocked** 震驚的
7. **weak** [wi:k] (a.) 虛弱的
8. **ugly** [`ʌgli] (a.) 醜陋的
9. **care about** 關心；在乎
10. **nothing** [`nʌθɪŋ] (n.) 無事

28

"This is terrible[1]," he thought.

"I really am an old, ugly tree. I want to go back[2] to my dark, lonely room. My life in the forest really was the best. I wasted[3] my life.

I always wished for[4] something more interesting. I never enjoyed the simple things in my life. Now, it is over[5]. There is nothing I can do."

1. **terrible** [`terəbəl] (a.) 恐怖的
2. **go back** 回到……去
3. **waste** [weɪst] (v.) 浪費
4. **wish for** 渴望
5. **over** [`oʊvər] (a.) 結束的
6. **gardener** [`gɑ:rdnər] (n.) 園丁；花匠
7. **groan** [groʊn] (v.) 呻吟
8. **chop** [tʃɑ:p] (v.) 劈；砍
9. **place** [pleɪs] (v.) 放置
10. **burn** [bɜ:rn] (v.) 燃燒；焚燒
11. **flame** [fleɪm] (n.) 火焰
12. **regret** [rɪ`gret] (n.) 懊悔

Soon, the gardener[6] came with an ax.
"This really is the end," groaned[7] the tree.

He chopped[8] the poor Fir tree into many pieces. Then, he placed[9] each piece into a fire. The poor tree burned[10] in the flames[11].

As he burned, he could see the children playing. They were playing with his golden star.

But it was too late for regrets[12] now.

Comprehension Quiz Chapter Two

A Fill in the blanks with the antonyms of the words underlined.

❶ The Fir tree was put into a ____________ room.
⇔ small

❷ His branches were ____________.
⇔ strong

❸ I will be ____________ next time.
⇔ careless

❹ It was too ____________ for regrets now.
⇔ early

B True or False.

T F ❶ The mice never got tired of listening to his stories.

T F ❷ The tree spent many lonely nights in a dark room.

T F ❸ A child took the star from the tree.

T F ❹ The tree didn't want to go back to the forest.

Appendixes

1. Basic Grammar
2. Guide to Listening Comprehension
3. Listening Guide
4. Listening Comprehension

Appendix

1 Basic Grammar

要增強英文閱讀理解能力，應練習找出英文的主結構。
要擁有良好的英語閱讀能力，首先要理解英文的段落結構。

英文的閱讀理解從「分解文章」開始

英文的文章是以「有意義的詞組」（指帶有意義的語句）所構成的。用（／）符號來區別各個意義語塊，請試著掌握其中的意義。

某樣東西（人、事、物）　如何做

He runs (very fast).
他 跑 （非常快）

It is raining.
雨 正在下

主詞　動詞　補語　（補充的話）

某樣東西（人、事、物）　如何做　怎麼樣

This is a cat.
這 是 一隻貓。

The cat is very big.
那隻貓 是 非常 大

主詞　動詞　受詞

某樣東西（人、事、物）　如何做　什麼

人，事物，兩者皆是受詞

I like you.
我 喜歡 你。

You gave me some flowers.
你 給 我 一些花

主詞　動詞　受詞　補語

某樣東西（人、事、物）　如何做　什麼　怎麼樣／什麼

You make me happy.
你 使（讓）我 幸福（快樂）

I saw him running.
我 看到 他 跑

其他修飾語或副詞等，都可以視為為了完成句子而臨時、額外、特別附加的，閱讀起來便可更加輕鬆；先具備這些基本概念，再閱讀《聖誕故事》的部分精選篇章，最後做了解文章整體架構的練習。

Della didn't wait.
黛拉 沒有等

She didn't want to lose her courage.
她 不想 失去 她的勇氣

She thought about her husband and his present.
她 想到 關於她丈夫和給他的禮物

She walked up the stairs, and saw a large woman.
她 走上 樓梯 並 看到 一個高大的女人

She looked very cold and unwelcoming .
她 看起來 非常冷酷且冷淡

Della asked her , "Will you buy my hair?"
黛拉 問 她 妳會買我的頭髮嗎

The woman looked at her and said ,
女人 看著 她 並 說

"I buy hair .
我 買 頭髮

Take off your hat .
脫下 妳的帽子

I need to see your hair."
我 得 看 妳的頭髮

So Della took off her hat , and pulled down her hair .
於是黛拉 脫下 她的帽子 並 放下 她的頭髮

It looked like a waterfall of beautiful hair.
它 看起來 像瀑布的美麗秀髮

"Twenty dollars," said Madame.
二十元 女士說

"I 'll give you twenty dollars for it."
我 會給 妳 二十元 買它

"Okay," said Della.
好的 黛拉說

" Cut it off quickly."
把它剪下來 快一點

Madame Sofronie cut off Della's hair ,
蘇富妮夫人 剪下 黛拉的頭髮

and gave her twenty dollars .
並 給 她 二十元
Della left the store happily.
黛拉 離開 這家店 開心地
She went out to buy Jim’s Christmas present.
她 走出 去買吉姆的聖誕禮物
For two hours, she searched many stores .
花了兩個小時 她 尋找 許多店
Finally, she found her husband’s present .
終於 她 找到 她丈夫的禮物
There was only one like it.
是 只有一件 像它一樣
It was very simple but elegant .
它 是 非常簡單但是高雅
It was a platinum fob chain for his watch.
它 是 一副白金錶鍊 配他的手錶
It was the perfect gift .
它 是 最完美的禮物
She paid twenty-one dollars for it.
她 付 二十元 為了它
She had no regrets .
她 有 不後悔
Jim would love it .
吉姆 會喜愛 它
Jim loved his watch .
吉姆 很愛 他的錶

Appendix 2

Guide to Listening Comprehension

When listening to the story, use some of the techniques shown below. If you take time to study some phonetic characteristics of English, listening will be easier.

Get in the flow of English.

English creates a rhythm formed by combinations of strong and weak stress intonations. Each word has its particular stress that combines with other words to form the overall pattern of stress or rhythm in a particular sentence.

When you are speaking and listening to English, it is essential to get in the flow of the rhythm of English. It takes a lot of practice to get used to such a rhythm. So, you need to start by identifying the stressed syllable in a word.

Listen for the strongly stressed words and phrases.

In English, key words and phrases that are essential to the meaning of a sentence are stressed louder. Therefore, pay attention to the words stressed with a higher pitch. When listening to an English recording for the first time, what matters most is to listen for a general understanding of what you hear. Do not try to hear every single word. Most of the unstressed words are articles or auxiliary verbs, which don't play an important role in the general context. At this level, you can ignore them.

Pay attention to liaisons.

In reading English, words are written with a space between them. There isn't such an obvious guide when it comes to listening to English. In oral English, there are many cases when the sounds of words are linked with adjacent words.

For instance, let's think about the phrase "**take off**," which can be used in "take off your clothes." "Take off your clothes" doesn't sound like [teɪk ɔ:f] with each of the words completely and clearly separated from the others. Instead, it sounds as if almost all the words in context are slurred together, [ˋteɪkɔ:f], for a more natural sound.

Shadow the voice of the native speaker.

Finally, you need to mimic the voice of the native speaker. Once you are sure you know how to pronounce all the words in a sentence, try to repeat them like an echo. Listen to the book again, but this time you should try a fun exercise while listening to the English.

This exercise is called "shadowing." The word "shadow" means a dark shade that is formed on a surface. When used as a verb, the word refers to the action of following someone or something like a shadow. In this exercise, pretend you are a parrot and try to shadow the voice of the native speaker.

Try to mimic the reader's voice by speaking at the same speed, with the same strong and weak stresses on words, and pausing or stopping at the same points.

Experts have already proven this technique to be effective. If you practice this shadowing exercise, your English speaking and listening skills will improve by leaps and bounds. While shadowing the native speaker, don't forget to pay attention to the meaning of each phrase and sentence.

Listen to what you want to shadow many times. Start out by just trying to shadow a few words or a sentence.

Mimic the CD out loud. You can shadow everything the speaker says as if you are singing a round, or you also can speak simultaneously with the recorded voice of the native speaker.

As you practice more, try to shadow more. For instance, shadow a whole sentence or paragraph instead of just a few words.

Appendix 3

Listening Guide

The Gift of the Magi

Chapter One page 18 29

Della sat (❶) ( ) kitchen table. She was counting something. "One penny, two pennies, three pennies . . .," she (❷). She was saving pennies. Now, she had one dollar and (❸)-seven cents.

❶ **at her:** at 後面緊接著 her，her 的 [h] 音會自動消失變成連音，通常以 h 開頭的代名詞，如 her、him、his 等，依前後文迅速發弱音時，[h] 音會略過而聽不清楚。

❷ **counted:** 重音在第一音節，count 的動詞原形 -t 音本為輕音，但是 counted 增加了 -ed 後，發音變成 [kaʊntɪd]，[t] 音較原來更清楚。

❸ **eighty:** -t- 原本發無聲的 [t] 音，但是 -t- 後面的 y 為有聲音，故使得 -ty 的發音變得更接近 [di] 的發音。

以下為《聖誕故事》各章節的前半部。一開始若能聽清楚發音，之後就沒有聽力的負擔。先聽過摘錄的章節，之後再反覆聆聽括弧內單字的發音，並仔細閱讀各種發音的說明。以下都是以英語的典型發音為基礎，所做的簡易說明，即使這裡未提到的發音，也可以配合音檔反覆聆聽，如此一來聽力必能更上層樓。

Chapter Two page 30 30

Della didn't wait. She didn't (❶) ( ) lose her courage. She (❷) ( ) her husband and his (❸). She (❹) ( ) the stairs and saw a large woman. She looked very cold and unwelcoming. Della asked her, "Will you buy my hair?"

❶ **want to:** want 的 t 和 to 的 t 連在一起發音，此時 to 的音聽起來就像 [tl̩]，在英語中若相同的兩個音連在一起時只需發音一次。

❷ **thought about:** about 的重音在 -bout 上，所以在日常會話中，a- 的音往往發得相當弱，聽起來若有似無，可由前後文判斷正確單字。

❸ **present:** 重音在第一音節，-s- 原本發無聲的 [s] 音，但是因為受到後面 [ə] 音的影響，會變成發 [z] 的有聲音。

❹ **walked up:** walked 發音為 [wɜ:kt]，和另一個字 worked（發音 [wɜ:rkt]）相當類似，必須仔細辨別所發的究竟是 [ɜ:] 或 [ɜ:r] 音。

Chapter Three page 42 31

Now, Jim (❶) ( ) his wife. He said, "Come here. I want to (❷) ( )." Della (❸) ( ) her husband and they held each for a few moments. "Please don't misunderstand me," he said. "Nothing could (❹) me from loving you. No haircut will change that."

❶ **looked at:** looked 的 -ed 接在 k 後面，發無聲的音，正確發音為 [lukt]。

❷ **hold you:** you 前面如果接了一個 [t] 的音，會與此 [t] 音形成連音，而發 [dʒ] 的音。

❸ **walked to:** walked 的 -ed 發 [t] 音，再接著其後的 to，兩個 [t] 只發音一次，故口語中聽起來與 walk to 的發音相同，需以上下文判斷時態。

❹ **stop:** k、p、t 等字母若接在 s 之後，這些子音會發成有聲音，聽起來類似 [g]、[b]、[d] 的音。

The Fir Tree

Chapter One page 56 32

Just outside a village, there was a beautiful (❶). It was full of so many (❷) ( ) trees. On the edge of the forest, there was a pretty Fir tree. He was still a small tree. He (❸) ( ) a very nice place. There was (❹) ( ) ( ) sunshine and fresh air.

❶ **forest:** 重音在第一音節，-st 的發音是 [st]，兩個無聲子音連在一起時會迅速略過，平順地發音。

❷ **kinds of:** kinds 與 of 連在一起發音，聽起來像是一個單字，of 前面的單字若是以子音結束，通常會變成連音，而 of 的 f 則發成 [v] 的音。

❸ **lived in:** lived 的 -ed 與 in 像一個單字連在一起發音，現在式 live in 會發出像 living 的連音，因屬於時常出現的發音型態，讀者應熟記此類發音法。

❹ **a lot of:** a lot of 中的 of 與前面的 lot 形成連音，而 t 則發成介於 [t] 與 [d] 之間的有聲音。

Chapter Two page 74 (33)

The Fir (❶) was put into a large room. He looked around the room curiously. Soon after, many servants and young girls came in. They (❷) ( ) decorate the tree. They hung many colored decorations on the tree. On the top, they put a large golden star.

❶ **tree:** tree 的音標為 [triː]，請注意與 three 的發音差別。

❷ **started to:** started 的 -ed 和 to 連著一起發音，to 的發音很輕，聽起來類似 [tə] 音。在一段文字中，基本上意義較不重要的助動詞、代名詞或介系詞等，聽起來發音會比較弱。

Appendix

4 Listening Comprehension

The Gift of the Magi

34 **A** Listen to the CD and circle the correct answer.

1. Jim said, "I sold the watch to buy your **(corns/combs)**."
2. Della looked at her **(hair/air)** in the mirror.
3. Della **(cried at/cry that)** her kitchen table.

35 **B** Listen to the CD and fill in the blanks with correct words.

1. Della's husband came home from __________ .
2. Della sat at the kitchen table, ________ money.
3. Jim gave Della a package ________ ________.

36 **C** Choose the correct answer.

1. ____?

   (a) A fob chain and hair combs.

   (b) Their apartment and kitchen table.

   (c) His watch and her very long hair.

   (d) Curling irons and a mirror.

The Fir Tree

37 **A** True or False.

T F ❶ ________________________________

T F ❷ ________________________________

T F ❸ ________________________________

38 **B** Listen to the CD and choose the correct answer.

❶ ________________________________?

(a) A much more interesting life.

(b) To become a small tree.

(c) To live in a peaceful forest.

(d) To listen to many stories.

❷ ________________________________?

(a) To keep him safe.

(b) To tell stories to the mice.

(c) Because they wanted to plant him in the spring.

(d) Because they didn't need him anymore.

Translation

聖誕禮物

作者簡介

p. 4

歐・亨利（William S. Porter "O. Henry"，1862–1910）是個高產的美國短篇小說作家，擅於製造出人意料的結尾，以筆名「歐・亨利」更廣為人知。據說，這名字是他經常對家貓喚「噢！亨利！」而來。

歐・亨利於 1862 年 9 月 11 日生於美國北卡羅來納州，並在此度過童年。三歲時，母親去世，他便受外婆與姑姑扶養長大。他唯一受過的正式教育是在姑姑莉娜的學校，並在這兒培養出對文學的終生熱愛。

歐・亨利對閱讀具有熱忱，但在 15 歲時離開學校，隨後移居德州，數年間從事各種不同的工作以維持生計，包括藥劑師、繪圖員、記者和出納員。

1897 年，歐・亨利因為銀行帳目問題被判處五年徒刑。1898 年，他進入俄亥俄州哥倫布的監獄服刑，根據自身經歷，開始短篇小說書寫。

三年間創作十幾篇短篇小說後，他在監獄裡成為「歐・亨利」，以掩蔽真實身分。1901 年 7 月 24 日出獄後，他隨即在紐約市定居，成為全職作家。僅僅十年間，他寫作超過 300 篇短篇小說，受國際讚譽為美國最愛的短篇小說家。

正如著名故事《最後一片葉子》（*The Last Leaf*）和《聖誕禮物》（*The Gift of the Magi*）裡可見，歐・亨利時常刻畫美國南方與紐約貧民窟裡，窮苦百姓的生活悲歡。而他故事最具代表性的特質，是在諷刺或巧合之下發生的劇情反轉。

故事簡介

p. 5

《聖誕禮物》是關於一對貧窮愛侶的聖誕故事。他們想送一份特別的聖誕禮物給對方，然而因為不夠錢而各自決定變賣私人物品。妻子剪去她引以為傲的頭髮換錢，買了錶鍊給丈夫；丈夫典當他珍重的金錶，買了妝飾妻子秀髮的髮飾。

故事標題 *The Gift of the Magi* 裡的 Magi，指的是耶穌出生時，帶來禮物的東方三賢士（Three Wise Men）。藉由閱讀故事，人們能夠思考聖誕節的真正精神，和那暗中犧牲珍寶換取禮物的夫妻兩人之間的愛。這意味著東方三賢士的行為，而他們本身也因此成了賢士。

樅樹

作者簡介

p. 6

1805 年 4 月 2 日，漢斯・克里斯汀・安徒生出生於歐登塞菲英島上的一個小漁村，雖然父親是名窮困的鞋匠，但識字且喜愛閱讀，思想先進的他鼓勵安徒生去培養藝術方面的興趣。

安徒生在大學時代開始寫作，他的第一本小說《即興詩人》（*The Improvisatore*），以 1833 年的義大利之旅作為背景，出版甫獲好評。

第一本童話故事《講給孩子們聽的故事》（*Tales Told for Children*）出版後，他以作家身分收獲更高的名聲，之後便成了人人喜愛的兒童文學大師。1875 年逝世前，他出版了約 130 個故事。

安徒生的眾多著作被視為兒童文學的傑作，如《小美人魚》、《醜小鴨》和《國王的新衣》。儘管遭遇諸多困難，安徒生克服了重重挑戰，為我們訴說了令人著迷的故事。

在安徒生的作品中，可看見抒情的寫作風格，透過美麗幻想世界和人道主義的展現，熱烈地交織融合。

安徒生終生未娶，最後隻身離世。葬禮之日，丹麥舉國身著喪服，國王與王后也出席他的葬禮。安徒生也是個活躍的詩人，而他美麗的詩作與童話故事至今仍深受世人喜愛。

故事簡介

p. 7

《樅樹》講述一棵永不滿足、需求無度的小樅樹的故事。

長久以來，他渴望離開無聊的森林，終於願望成真後，他變成了一棵聖誕樹，在聖誕夜晚享盡璀璨富麗。

然而聖誕節過後，小樅樹卻被遺棄在閣樓裡。隨著時光流逝，他越發孤單。

一天，小樅樹了悟到，原來那段平淡愜意的森林生活才是他最快樂的時光，他發誓要更加珍惜眼前微小的幸福，可惜一切都太遲了。

這篇童話故事以寓言形式，教導我們生命中微小的真理。

聖誕禮物

[第一章] 一元八角七分

p. 18–19 黛拉坐在廚房的餐桌前數著:「一分錢，兩分錢，三分錢⋯⋯」

之前她就一直在存錢，現在，她手上有一元八角七分錢，這是她努力省下來的，每回她到雜貨店總是會說：「喔，這太貴了，麻煩你幫我打個折。」她就這麼過了好幾個月。

現在她數著這些省下來的錢，一遍又一遍，但就只有一元八角七分，她忍不住大喊：「不可能！應該有更多錢才對，我存了那麼久了！」

p. 20–21 黛拉生活並不富裕，她住在一間很小的公寓裡，一星期房租要八元，她要聰明地使用每一分錢才行。

公寓的入口有個門鈴，已經壞了很久，門口還有一個信箱，不過小到沒辦法收信，這公寓實在是糟透了。

在信箱的上方寫著：「詹姆斯・迪林漢・揚先生」，這是黛拉的先生。

很久以前，詹姆斯・迪林漢・揚先生對自己的姓名非常自豪，當時他每週的薪水有 30 元，現在卻只剩下 20 元，根本買不了多少東西。

不過，有時這對他不算什麼大不了的事，因為他一回到家，妻子就會出來迎接，給他一個擁抱，他是黛拉口中的「吉姆」。

p. 22–23 這時黛拉依然坐在廚房餐桌前哭泣著，她擦乾淚水，站起身。

明天就是聖誕節了，她卻只有一元八角七分可以買聖誕禮物送給丈夫，存了那麼久的錢還是不夠，本來黛拉想買個很棒的禮物的。

她走向另一扇窗，經過了一面鏡子，就放在兩扇窗之間，當然，這並不是太好的鏡子，只是一面放在每週租金八元公寓裡的鏡子。她看著鏡中的自己，雙眼都哭紅腫了。

p. 24–25 一個想法突然跳進她腦中。原本她的頭髮是綁起來的，現在她將頭髮放下來。她有著一頭長而美麗的秀髮。有兩樣東西是她和丈夫非常珍惜的。

其中一樣是一支金錶，那是吉姆的祖父留給他的，他很珍視那支錶。

另一樣就是黛拉的頭髮，許多人都羨慕她那一頭長髮，甚至有人對她說：「妳的頭髮比席巴女王珍藏的珠寶還要美呢。」

吉姆的金錶同樣受人讚嘆，有人告訴他：「你的錶太棒了，國王都會戴在身上呢。」

也因此，吉姆和黛拉對於擁有這兩樣東西非常驕傲。

p. 26–27 黛拉依舊看著自己的頭髮，順著肩膀滑落在後背，一直延伸到膝蓋，好長好長，長得都快像條裙子了。

她很快把頭髮又綁起來，但卻突然感到一陣悲傷，串串淚珠滾落雙頰。

她迅速穿上破舊的棕色大衣，戴上棕色舊帽子，鎖上公寓大門，衝下樓走出公寓大廈來到街上，去找一家非常特別的店。

沒幾分鐘她便找到了，看到招牌上寫著：「蘇富妮夫人美髮用品店。」

[第二章] 聖誕禮物

p. 30–31　黛拉毫不遲疑。她不想失去勇氣，心裡只想著丈夫和送他的禮物。

她走上樓梯，看到一個肥胖的女人，看起來很冷酷，不太歡迎她的樣子。

黛拉問她：「妳願意買我的頭髮嗎？」

那女人看著她說：「我買，先把帽子脫下來，我要看看妳的頭髮。」

於是黛拉脫下帽子，放下如飛瀑般美麗的秀髮。

「二十元。」蘇富妮夫人說：「我出二十元買妳的頭髮。」

「好，」黛拉回答：「快動手吧！」蘇富妮夫人剪下黛拉的長髮，給了她二十元。

p. 32–33　黛拉愉快地離開店裡，去買吉姆的聖誕禮物。

她找了兩小時，找遍各個商店，終於找到了送給丈夫的禮物了，它獨一無二，設計簡單卻高雅，一條適合吉姆那只金錶的白金錶鍊。

這真是個完美的禮物，她花了二十一塊元買下它，心裡完全不後悔。吉姆一定會很喜歡，因為他很愛那只錶。

不過這幾天他卻表現得有些不自在，只在私下偷偷看錶，那是因為錶上繫著的皮帶太老舊了。

不過現在，他可以抬頭挺胸地看錶，再也不用覺得尷尬了。

p. 34–35 黛拉帶著她的錶鍊和八角七分趕回家，突然對失去頭髮感到有些難過，不過她想：「很快就會長回來的。」

她拿出她的捲髮棒，把短髮弄成許多小捲，一遍又一遍看著鏡中的頭髮。

「希望吉姆不會討厭我現在的髮型才好。」她想。

「我這麼做是為了他，是為了愛。只有一元八角七分能買些什麼呢？不對！吉姆一定不會討厭的，他會覺得我像合唱團的女孩。」

所以，她忘了頭髮的事，開始準備晚餐。今天晚上他們的晚餐是豬排和咖啡。

p. 36 黛拉聽到吉姆走上公寓樓梯的聲音，他一直都很準時回家。

她趕緊選了一張靠近門口的椅子坐下，把錶鍊拿在手中，暗自祈禱著：「拜託讓他覺得我還是很美麗吧！」

門打開，她的丈夫走了進來，他今晚看起來非常疲累，才二十二歲的他看起來卻不只這個年紀，因為有太多事要操心了。

吉姆脫下舊外套，他實在該換件新的了。他看著妻子，面無表情，黛拉想：「他在想些什麼？他不喜歡我的髮型嗎？他覺得我這樣很醜嗎？」

p. 38–39 黛拉等不及吉姆開口，便跳起來衝向他。

「吉姆，親愛的！你怎麼不說話？別露出那副表情，頭髮很快就會長出來的，別擔心，它長得很快！」她說。

「妳把頭髮剪了？」吉姆問她。他似乎反應有些遲鈍，其實一眼就可以看出黛拉剪短了頭髮。

「是啊。」她說：「我剪了頭髮拿去賣，幫你買了一個很棒的禮物，我知道你一定會很喜歡，是個最適合你的禮物。你不喜歡我的髮型嗎？我還是原來的我啊，你會因為有沒有頭髮就不愛我了嗎？」

[第三章] 最大的驚喜

p. 42–43 現在吉姆看著妻子說：「過來這裡，我想抱抱妳。」

黛拉走到丈夫身邊，兩人擁抱了好一會兒。

「不要誤會我的意思，」他說：「我不會因為任何事而不愛妳，即使妳換了髮型也不會。」

接著他看了看口袋，把裡面的東西拿出來放在桌上。

「把盒子打開，」吉姆說：「妳就會明白為什麼為會這麼奇怪了，去吧，把它打開。」

她拿起盒子把它拆開。不一會兒，她立刻開心地大喊：「啊，親愛的！好漂亮啊。」這股快樂的心情馬上化作眼淚，黛拉哭了起來。

p. 44–45 她的丈夫立刻衝到她身邊。「不要哭，」他說：「不要哭。」

但她就是淚流不止，吉姆在身邊安慰了她一會兒。

放在桌上的是一組髮釵，看起來漂亮極了。黛拉上次在百老匯的商店櫥窗見到後，便一直很想要，不過價格實在太貴了，要是別在她褐色的長髮上一定很美。

她拿起髮釵緊擁著，開心地看著丈夫說道：「我很快就可以用了，我的頭髮長得很快。」

接著她突然想到。「喔！對了！」她大喊：「我還沒把禮物拿給你。」

她跳起來張開手，眼神布滿喜悅的光芒。

p. 46–47 「這很美吧！配你的錶正合適。我今天到處找才找到的，現在你不用因為那只錶覺得尷尬了，可以每天拿出來看個上百次。把錶給我，我幫你裝上去。」她說。

不過吉姆並沒有把錶給她，反而走到沙發坐下，微笑著。

「黛拉，」他說：「我現在不想去管聖誕節或什麼聖誕禮物，先別提這些了吧，以後再說吧。」

「我的錶已經不在身上了，我把它賣掉買了妳的髮釵。現在妳可以先去準備晚餐嗎？」

黛拉就這麼望著他，簡直不敢相信，不過她什麼也沒說，默默走到廚房去準備晚餐。

p. 48–49 人們通常習慣在聖誕節送禮物，這個傳統是由東方三賢士留下的，他們是三位智者，很久以前他們為出生在馬槽的耶穌帶來一份禮物，他們是智者，帶來的禮物就是智慧。

本篇是兩個愚人的故事，他們傻傻的放棄了最珍貴的事物，但他們這麼做是為了愛，而愛正是我們送禮的理由。

所以他們是兩個最傻的聰明人，他們就是智者，雖然貧窮，卻因愛而富有。他們為了彼此放棄自己最珍貴的東西，這正是聖誕節的真諦。

樅樹

[第一章] 森林裡的樹

p. 56–57 就在一個小村落外，有一座美麗的森林，生長著各式各樣的樹木。

在森林邊緣，有一棵華美的樅樹。它現在還只是一棵小樹，長在一片豐沃的土地上，每天有曬不完的太陽與新鮮空氣。

小樅樹旁還圍繞著許許多多的樅樹，有些比它大得多，有些就和它一般大小。還有很多松樹，看起來是如此高大，小樅樹希望自己也能像它們一樣。

小樅樹過著挺不錯的生活，但它卻不自覺，它根本不在乎溫暖的陽光或是新鮮的空氣。

p. 58–59 許多孩童會來森林裡摘草莓，有時候他們會坐在小樅樹下，也往往會說：「我們去坐在那棵小樅樹下吧，它真是美麗。」

可是小樅樹一點兒也不喜歡，他不希望自己是「小」樅樹。

每一年，樅樹都會慢慢長大，但是它卻還是開心不起來，他看看圍繞在身邊的其他樹木。

他心想：「我想要長得和那些樹一樣高大，我要枝葉茂密、高大挺拔，從空中俯瞰一切事物，我要鳥兒在我枝頭築巢，也想要在風中優雅地彎腰。」

它從不覺得快樂。

p. 60–61 兩年過去了，小樅樹不斷不斷地長大，現在它比以前高大許多了。

「我慢慢長大了，」它想：「再長大一點吧，我還要長得更高。」

每年秋天，樵夫會來這兒砍下最高大的樹。小樅樹聽見了「砍！砍！砍！」的聲音，接著，一陣巨大的碰撞聲，一棵大樹應聲倒下，這時小樅樹感到十分驚恐。

它想：「人類為什麼要砍這些樹？它們會被帶去哪裡？會發生什麼事呢？」

p. 62–63 小樅樹看到幾隻燕子，便提出它心中的疑問。

「是啊，我有見過它們，」燕子回答：「我曾飛到埃及去，看到許多大船，船上都有巨大的船桅，船桅上掛著白色巨帆，在空中飛舞著，高雅得很，你應該感到驕傲。」

小樅樹一聽開心極了，心想：「我想要在海上航行，我想要做巨大高挺的船桅，旁邊還有帆布飛舞，我也想要過得那麼開心。」

空氣與陽光聽到了小樅樹的話，對它說道：「別羨慕人家的生活，現在就要開開心心的，你有溫暖的陽光，還有健康的枝幹呢。」

但是小樅樹並不理解它們的話。

p. 64 今年，樵夫在聖誕節前來到了森林，但是卻不砍那些高大的樹木，反而是砍些年輕的小樹。

小樅樹覺得好奇怪，「他們為什麼要砍這麼年輕的小樹呢？」

一些小麻雀正停在小樅樹枝頭，於是他便問麻雀：「這些樹會到哪兒去？它們都比我還小，那些人為什麼要砍呢？」

p. 66–67 這回麻雀回答：「我們知道！我們從村莊窗戶往屋裡瞧，這些樹都被送到那裡，它們會被裝飾得很美，有好多五顏六色的燈光，它們會過得很幸福，住在溫暖的屋裡，腳邊還放著很多禮物。」

小樅樹聽得津津有味，心想：「這聽起來真棒，比在海上航行更好，我也想要住在那樣的地方，我在這片森林裡實在太痛苦了，更美好的生活正在等著我呢。」

陽光與空氣又再次聽到它的心聲，便對小樅樹說：「別傻了，在森林裡的生活是最棒的，要開開心心在這裡生活。」不過小樅樹對它們的勸告聽而不聞。

p. 69 終於，樵夫們靠過來了，他們站在小樅樹面前說：「這一棵太完美了！」

過了一會兒，小樅樹感到一陣劇烈的痛苦，是一把斧頭，在它身上砍！砍！砍！

小樅樹跌落在地。砰！

這並不如它夢想般美好，剎時它感到一陣失落！

小樅樹想著：「我的家！我馬上要離開家，再也無法回來，再也無法感受新鮮的空氣與溫暖的陽光，再也無法聽見鳥兒歌唱，真是讓人太感傷了！」

[第二章] 悲慘的生活

p. 74 小樅樹被放到一間大屋裡，它好奇地環視四周，沒多久，許多僕人和年輕女孩走了進來。

他們開始裝飾小樅樹，在它身上掛著五顏六色的裝飾品，樹頂則是放上一個大大的金色星星。

樅樹看著自己的枝幹被裝飾得繽紛多彩，看起來非常美麗。

「從現在起我就要過著很棒的新生活了，」小樅樹想：「我會住在這間溫暖的屋子裡，陽光和空氣都說錯了，說不定麻雀會來看我，還會對其他樹木說我過著了不起的生活。」

它現在滿懷開心，對未來充滿了信心。

p. 76–77 又過了一會兒，房門被打開，許多孩子跑了進來。

他們跑到樅樹前停了下來，後面跟著幾個大人，大伙全都一起欣賞著這棵美麗的樹，小樅樹覺得非常開心。

那天晚上，房裡喧鬧不已，孩子們開心地喊叫，圍著樅樹手舞足蹈。

接著所有的人一起唱聖誕歌曲，樅樹看著這一切滿心陶醉，心想：「這全都是因為我呢！以後每晚我都會享受這一切。」它內心感到無比滿足。

p. 78–79 第二天清晨，樅樹想要再見到孩子們，但是他們卻一直沒來看它，反倒有幾個僕人走進房裡。

小樅樹心想：「昨天僕人們把我裝飾好，今天他們還會幫我打扮打扮吧。」但是卻什麼也沒有發生。

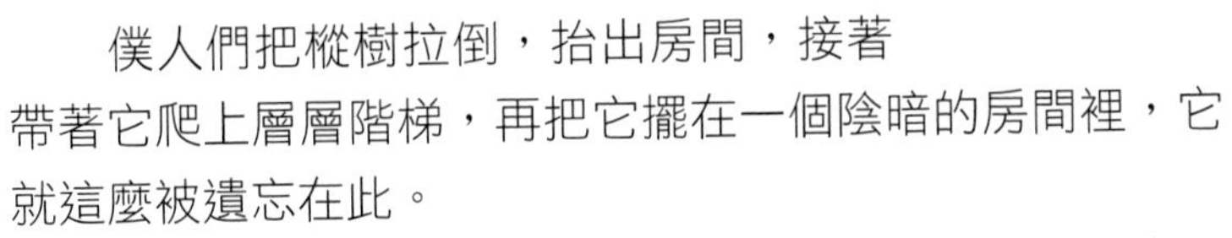

僕人們把樅樹拉倒，抬出房間，接著帶著它爬上層層階梯，再把它擺在一個陰暗的房間裡，它就這麼被遺忘在此。

無數個寂寞的夜晚消逝，一天夜裡，四周突然冒出一點聲音。

「吱吱！吱吱！」是小老鼠發出的聲音，好奇的小老鼠想要認識認識小樅樹，於是它告訴老鼠們森林裡的點點滴滴故事。

小老鼠個個驚異不已，說道：「你的生活真是有趣！你在森林過得好幸福喔！」

小樅樹回答：「沒錯，我在森林裡時的確很開心，但是我現在的生活已經不再有趣了。」

p. 80–81 到了夜裡，牠們又跑去聽小樅樹說故事，一連幾夜，它說了許許多多關於聖誕夜的故事給老鼠聽。最後，樅樹再也沒有故事可說，只能不斷重複相同的故事。

老鼠們心想：「這些故事畢竟不是那麼有趣。」

接著夜裡老鼠便不再去找小樅樹了。

它在那個陰暗的房裡感到非常寂寞。

「老鼠為什麼不來找我了呢？」它想：「牠們來聽我說故事的日子有趣多了，我要再過那種快樂的日子，下次我一定要注意一點，等我離開這間屋子的時候，我要好好享受每件事物，但是還要等多久呢？」

p. 82–83 有一天，這間灰暗、寂寞的房間門被打開了，一大群人走了進來。

「終於，」樅樹心想：「他們來帶給我新生活了。」

其中一個男人靠近，把它推倒在地。唉唷！小樅樹重重地跌在地上，接著兩名僕人把它抬出屋外。

如今，小樅樹又再度躺在陽光下。

「這真是太美好了，我的新生活即將展開，現在已經是春天，他們會把我種在土裡讓我重新生長。」

小樅樹開心地享受著新鮮的空氣，它環視花園，實在是美極了，玫瑰與康乃馨花兒綻放，還有許多鳥兒在花園裡飛舞，好個美妙的一天。

p. 84–85 小樅樹在陽光下放鬆心情，盡情伸展枝幹。

就在這時，小樅樹才突然發現一件駭人的事。它無法移動枝葉，往身上瞧了瞧，霎時驚訝不已，它的枝葉全都已枯黃，枝幹也變得脆弱，現在它成了一棵悲慘的樹。

一群孩子在花園裡四處奔跑，喊著：「看！是那棵聖誕樹，好舊好醜喔，不過那顆金色星星還掛在上面！」

其中一個孩子把星星從小樅樹上拆下來，這些孩子們根本不在乎這棵乾枯的老樹，它身上沒有一處是美麗的。

p. 86–87 「這太可怕了！」小樅樹想。

「我現在成了棵醜陋的老樹了，我想回到那個黑暗孤獨的房裡。以前在森林裡的生活真是我最棒的日子了，而我卻浪費了生命，老想著過更有趣的生活，從未好好享受生活中最單純美好的一切，現在一切都完了！我再也無力做任何事了！」

這時園丁帶著斧頭出現。

「現在一切真的結束了。」小樅樹嘆息道。

園丁把小樅樹劈成許多塊，再把一塊塊木柴丟進爐火中，可憐的小樅樹便在火花裡燃盡生命。

它在火中燃燒時，還看見孩子們拿著那顆金色的星星在玩耍嬉戲。

但是現在一切都太遲了，後悔也來不及了！

Answers

P. 28 Ⓐ discount, love, tear, hair

Ⓑ ❶ -ⓔ ❷ -ⓒ ❸ -ⓑ
❹ -ⓐ ❺ -ⓓ

P. 29 Ⓒ ❶ F ❷ T ❸ F ❹ T ❺ F

Ⓓ ❶ valued ❷ loved ❸ envied

P. 40 Ⓐ ❶ walked ❷ took ❸ cut ❹ opened

Ⓑ ❶ saw ❷ sat ❸ couldn't wait

P. 41 Ⓒ ❶ (c) ❷ (a)

Ⓓ ❶ perfect ❷ dollars ❸ regrets
❹ embarrassed

P. 50 Ⓐ Christmas, three men, gift, wise

Ⓑ ❶ T ❷ F ❸ T ❹ F ❺ F

P. 51 Ⓒ ❶ was taking ❷ was growing
❸ wasn't giving ❹ was going

Ⓓ ❷ → ❹ → ❶ → ❸

P. 70 A ❶ pick ❷ sits ❸ cuts ❹ flies

B ❶ T ❷ T ❸ F ❹ F

P. 71 C ❶ many ❷ much ❸ much ❹ many

D ❷ → ❺ → ❹ → ❶ → ❸

P. 88 A ❶ large ❷ weak ❸ careful ❹ late

B ❶ F ❷ T ❸ T ❹ F

P. 102 A ❶ combs ❷ hair ❸ cried at

B ❶ work ❷ counting ❸ to open

C ❶ What were the two most valuable things to Jim and Della? (c)

P. 103 A ❶ There was a beautiful forest outside the village. (T)
❷ The small pine tree wanted to be big. (F)
❸ The woodcutters came to the forest to cut down trees. (T)

B ❶ What did the tree always dream of? (a)
❷ Why did the servants put the tree into the dark, lonely room? (d)

Adaptors of *The Christmas Stories*

Louise Benette

Macquarie University (MA, TESOL)
Sookmyung Women's University, English Instructor

David Hwang

Michigan State University (MA, TESOL)
Ewha Womans University, English Chief Instructor,
CEO at EDITUS

聖誕故事【二版】

The Christmas Stories

作者 _ 歐・亨利／安徒生
（O. Henry / Hans Christian Andersen）
改寫 _ Louise Benette, David Hwang
插圖 _ Ludmila Pipchenko
翻譯 / 編輯 _ 羅竹君
作者 / 故事簡介翻譯 _ 王采翎
校對 _ 王采翎
封面設計 _ 林書玉
排版 _ 葳豐／林書玉
播音員 _ Leo D. Schotz, Fiona Steward
製程管理 _ 洪巧玲
發行人 _ 周均亮
出版者 _ 寂天文化事業股份有限公司
電話 _ +886-2-2365-9739
傳真 _ +886-2-2365-9835
網址 _ www.icosmos.com.tw
讀者服務 _ onlineservice@icosmos.com.tw
出版日期 _ 2019年12月 二版一刷（250201）
郵撥帳號 _ 1998620-0 寂天文化事業股份有限公司

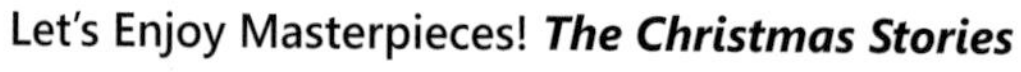

國家圖書館出版品預行編目資料

聖誕故事：聖誕禮物／樅樹 / O. Henry, Hans Christian Andersen 原著；Louise Benette, David Hwang 改寫 . -- 二版 . -- [臺北市] : 寂天文化 , 2019.12
面； 公分 . -- (Grade 1 經典文學讀本)
譯自 : The Christmas stories
ISBN 978-986-318-865-0(25K 平裝附光碟片)

1. 英語　2. 讀本

805.18　108019936